GOING THROUGH THE POTIONS

PACIFIC NORTH WITCHES MYSTERY #1

SAMANTHA SILVER

I stared right into the dragon's open mouth as it roared at me, and I gulped. His red and yellow scales glistened in the rays of sunlight that peeked through the canopy of the trees.

"He's just like a big old pussycat," I muttered to myself. "Good kitty."

Well, apart from the fact that when you had to get a collar off a cat, it was generally pretty easy to distract them with a treat and then quickly undo the collar before they realized what was happening.

Dragons, on the other hand, were a bit more of an issue. After all, this particular dragon's teeth were about the size of the average housecat. And then there's that whole fire-breathing thing, too.

This particular dragon had a large blue collar around his neck. A collar that I was supposed to get off without becoming a midmorning snack in the process.

I stepped to the right, keeping one eye on the collar and another on those giant teeth. The dragon was well aware that I was here and was absolutely not on board with what I was trying to do.

"*Rhea, mother of the gods, lull this dragon to sleep,*" I ordered, pulling out my wand and pointing it directly at the dragon. In a flash of color, however, the dragon leaped up toward the sky, causing the spell to miss, and I let out a gasp of surprise.

"Come on, don't you want a nice nap?" I called up to him when I'd gotten ahold of myself once more. "It's a nice, sunny day out. Perfect weather for a bit of a snooze!"

The dragon replied by shooting a burst of fire toward me, which I managed to avoid by casting a quick shield spell, protecting me from the flames. "I guess that's a no," I muttered.

The dragon spread his wings wide and began flying around the forest in a large circle. Great. I hated flying.

A broom lay on the ground nearby and I grabbed it, jumping up onto it and soaring into the sky. I gripped the handle tight as I flew toward the dragon, but I was at an innate disadvantage: I was a witch from an earth coven. I was most comfortable with my feet on the ground and my hands in a pile of dirt. The dragon, on the other hand, was in his element here in the sky. Flying was as natural as breathing for him. I had to change the odds.

"*Rhea, mother of the gods, turn me invisible,*" I ordered,

pointing my wand at myself. Straightaway, my body and broom disappeared from view. It might have been a little bit disconcerting for me—I wasn't a confident flyer when I knew where my body was, let alone when I couldn't see it—but it would have been worse for the dragon.

His long neck craned from side to side as he looked for me, vainly trying to figure out where I was while I flew toward him. Unable to determine my location, the dragon decided to take the nuclear option, which I wasn't expecting. He opened his mouth and breathed out flame, sending fire everywhere. And I mean *everywhere*. Some of the trees below caught fire as the flames hit them, but more importantly, he was also shooting fire toward me.

I spun sideways to avoid the flames, sending my broom shooting upward to get away from the fiery end the dragon had planned for me. I eventually found myself flying right above him, looking straight down at the blue collar that I had to remove.

I figured I probably had one shot at this.

I stuck my wand between my teeth so I could guide my broom with both hands as I shot straight down toward the dragon. When I was about a foot or two above him, I jumped off the broom, landing on the dragon's back, and immediately lunged for the collar.

Just as soon as I'd grabbed it with one hand, the dragon spun himself around, desperately trying to get me off his back.

4 | SAMANTHA SILVER

It took every ounce of willpower I had not to open my mouth and drop the wand as I found myself dangling in midair, one hand holding onto the collar while the rest of me hung powerlessly. I looked up and saw the clip. I reached for it, but the dragon took a sharp left, and the laws of physics meant my body moved to the side, so I couldn't reach the clip anymore. Not to mention, the grip my other hand had on the collar was failing.

There was no time to bother with the clip to release the collar. I wasn't going to be able to get to it, not with the dragon doing his best impression of a cheetah on cocaine as he tried to get me to fall off him. I grabbed my wand from my mouth and pointed it at the collar.

"Rhea, mother of the gods, slice through this collar."

Magic burst forth from my wand, and the next thing I knew, I was plummeting toward the ground. But hey, at least I had the collar in my hand. If I messed up this next spell I was probably going to die, but at least I would have succeeded.

"Rhea, mother of the gods, make me float gently to the Earth."

My plummet quickly turned into more of a soft flow, like a feather slowly falling from the sky. I could see Keith Rockway, the wizard currently judging my work, staring up at me from the field where we had started. His arms were crossed, and I happily waved the collar in his direction. The burning trees had been put out; Keith must have done that to prevent as much damage to the forest as possible.

A minute later my feet were on solid ground once more, and I raced over to the field where this test had started and threw the collar at Keith's feet.

"There it is." I looked up at him, a self-assured smirk on his face, but his reply came in the form of a slowly raised eyebrow. His brown eyes betrayed absolutely no emotion. Keith was a friend of my mom's and the head honcho of the magical fixers here at Mt. Rheanier. In his early fifties, he always said my antics as a child were most of the reason he had gone gray early.

Now, he was going to judge whether I passed the test to be allowed to study to become a magical fixer. After all, when I had completed my witches' exam—the examination every witch and wizard took upon coming of age to determine their magical skill levels and what occupation would be within their skillsets—I wasn't exactly the best student. I definitely didn't score highly enough to be given automatic entry into the magical fixer program, which was one of the most prestigious in the entire paranormal world. Magical fixers were basically general problem solvers. If you had an issue that involved magic to fix, you called the fixers. Their magical skills had to be top-of-the-line, since they dealt with anything and everything on a daily basis.

So, now that I was twenty-seven years old and more mature—in theory, anyway—I was taking a supplemental exam that would give me entry to the magical fixer program. The test had required me to get the collar off an angry dragon who would do his best to stop me.

"Here it is," I said, motioning to the collar as the dragon flew down next to me. It was suddenly surrounded by a white-hot flash of light, and when the light disappeared a second later, the dragon had shifted back into a six-foot-two blond man with messed-up hair and a carefree smile.

"You certainly gave me a run for my money there, Ali," he said with a grin. "I zigged and zagged so hard I almost made myself dizzy."

"Yeah, I was about ninety percent sure my arm was just going to detach from my shoulder completely," I replied. "But I got the collar in the end. So, do I pass?"

Keith looked at me. "No, absolutely not."

"What?" I complained. "Why not? I got the collar back."

"For one thing, you have the collar sliced in half. You should have unclipped it normally and brought it back in one piece, rather than destroying it to finish the task. Completing a task incorrectly is just as bad as not completing it at all."

"The rules didn't say I had to bring it back in one piece," I argued.

"And part of being a magical fixer means reading between the lines," Keith replied. "Besides, on top of that, there is the issue that your actions caused Blaze to set the forest on fire."

"So a few trees got burned."

"And what if that happened to property that belonged to the person you were supposed to be helping?"

"Well, if I were a magical fixer, I'd just fix it after," I replied, crossing my arms, and Keith sighed. I could practically *feel* him regretting ever being friends with my mom.

"Sorry, Althea," he said. Keith had always insisted on using my full name instead of calling me Ali like almost everyone else. "I'm afraid I can't accept you into the magical fixer education program."

CHAPTER 2

"This is bull," I said, kicking at a loose stone as Blaze and I walked back to town together. I had tried arguing with Keith some more, telling him that I totally deserved to be accepted into the program for my creative thinking and doing whatever was necessary to get the collar off the dragon, but he wasn't deterred. Apparently I didn't have the right "temperament" to be a magical fixer just yet, whatever that meant. It wasn't like I was a horse or something.

Unfortunately, Keith's word was law. And now I had to wait six more months before I could try again.

"For what it's worth, I thought your way of getting the collar was creative," Blaze said. "I've done this same test about ten times for Keith, and nine of them failed. You're actually the first one I've seen in the two years I've been doing this to actually succeed."

"See? All the more reason to let me into the program."

"Why do you want to be a magical fixer anyway? That doesn't seem to me to be very much your thing."

"I'm in it entirely for the money," I said. Being a magical fixer paid well, and my current job, being a plant collector for a major corporation here in the paranormal world, didn't.

"So much for doing it for a love of the work," Blaze grinned at me.

"Oh please, like you can talk. Your family is loaded."

"True."

While Blaze came from money, I most definitely didn't. My family wasn't exactly poor, but they weren't rich, either. And thanks to my less-than-stellar working habits as a young witch, I had never amounted to all that much, and now every morning I received an email telling me what plants the corporation needed and in what amounts. I had to take them to headquarters every afternoon, and for that I was paid just enough to pay my mom a pittance to stay in my childhood bedroom, pay for a bit of food, and not much else.

The sad reality of my current situation didn't stop me from having big dreams, though. I wanted to pay for a house for my mom. She had raised my sister and me all by herself after dad died when I was a child, and while it could be argued that I wasn't exactly a perennial winner of the world's best daughter award, I was grateful for her all the same. Besides, my sister was a regular nominee for the award, so maybe it was just me who was a bit messed up.

Despite working two jobs for most of her life just to make sure there was always enough for my sister and me, there was never much left over, and while she never complained, I wanted to make sure that my mom's later years were spent in relative comfort. A million abras would buy a gorgeous house by the lake here in Mt. Rheanier, and that was my goal.

The problem was, I was only making a hundred abras a day as a plant collector, and keeping even less of it. That was the inspiration for becoming a magical fixer. My salary would immediately jump to five hundred abras a day—abracadollars were the currency used in the magical world—and that would make it much, much easier for me to save up the kind of money I needed.

It might even allow me to get my own place. Because as much as I loved my mom, I also loved privacy, and not hearing about how I needed to find myself a good wizard and settle down on a regular basis. And, of course, there was also my grandmother. But the less said about her, the better.

"Are you going to try again in six months?" Blaze asked.

"Yeah. Does he use the same test the second time around?"

"I don't know," Blaze said thoughtfully. "I don't think I've ever seen the same witch or wizard come back twice."

I grinned. "What on earth do you do to them?"

"Well, one witch accidentally got caught in one of my flamethrowers. I stopped it immediately as soon as I realized, but she still spent two weeks in the hospital, with Healers putting salves all over her body."

"Yikes."

"A wizard who thought he was clever turned himself into a bird to try and catch me, and let's just say it was a bit of a Jonah and the whale situation."

I grinned. "At least you didn't swallow, I assume."

"Nope, but I don't think I've ever seen anyone as pale as him after he turned back into a wizard. Besides, I wouldn't have eaten the wizard, even as a crow. I'm a vegan."

I snickered at the idea of this big dragon shifter next to me being vegan, but hey, we were in the Pacific Northwest. Those sorts of things weren't exactly rare.

"So what are you doing for the rest of the day?" Blaze asked, and I shrugged.

"I guess I'm just going to go home and wallow in self-pity for a bit. You?"

"Meeting a friend for dinner. I'll see you around."

"Sure thing."

We reached the end of the path and Blaze took a left down the street and headed toward town. I stopped and stared after him for a minute, trying to decide exactly what I wanted to do. It was early October, and the temperature was still warm enough in the late afternoon that with a sweater on I could enjoy a nice walk by the lake.

It was certainly preferable to going home. I didn't want to tell my mom what had happened. I didn't even tell her I was trying out to become a magical fixer; I didn't want her to get her hopes up that her daughter might actually do something right with her life for a change. It turned out that was the right call.

Sighing, I turned away from the road and followed the single-track path that led toward Lake Cybele. About two minutes later, I was on the beach. There were a few people around, but not that many, and I made my way to a patch of grass away from the sand and sat down, looking at the calm lake water and gazing up at Mount Rheanier. Our little town—named for the mountain—sat at the base of the inactive volcano. Whenever I felt stressed, I always came to the beach. It was such a gorgeous sight, seeing the crystal blue waters of the lake, with the deep green trees of the forest in the background, the cute buildings of the town, and the mountain rising high above everything.

I couldn't believe I'd failed. I had thought that getting the collar at all costs had been the most important thing. I hadn't factored in that I had to do it while preventing any damage to the forest or to the collar itself. Maybe Keith was right. Maybe I didn't have the right attitude to be a magical fixer. I wasn't the sort of person who colored in the lines. I never had been. My sister, on the other hand, absolutely was.

Why couldn't I be perfect, like Leda?

I just wasn't wired that way. As the sun began to set, I walked along the pedestrian path back toward town. I didn't have a broom, so it took about thirty-five minutes, since I had to walk all the way along the perimeter of the lake before getting to the other side, where the town was built.

Mt. Rheanier was a small town with cute Germanic-style buildings built right up against the shore of the lake. The streets were cobbled and wide, with plenty of green spaces and parks everywhere. My mom lived in a small cottage that she rented on the outskirts of town, away from the lake. It was old—built about two hundred years ago when Mt. Rheanier was first settled by paranormals—and somewhat falling apart. I'd grown up in this two-bedroom cottage, and I now lived in a small converted shed at the back of the property. I was fairly certain if I still lived in the house I would have stabbed somebody by now.

Luckily, by the time I walked back, the sun had well and truly dipped over the horizon, and it was dark enough that I managed to make it to my shed without my mom spotting me through the window. I didn't really want to face her right now. I didn't want to have to hide my failure from her yet again. On the bright side, hiding from my mom after doing something wrong was something I was *very* used to.

I cooked myself a bowl of ramen for dinner—I liked to pretend adding fresh corn from the market made it healthy—and settled down on my bed in the corner of the room to sleep.

CHAPTER 3

I woke up early the next morning, enjoying the split second of ignorant bliss before the events of the previous day came flooding back to me. Maybe I wasn't meant to be a magical fixer after all. Maybe I should become a Healer instead. After all, that was what my mom had always hoped for. Althea *was* a goddess of healing.

Still, I didn't think there was any Healer program in the entire paranormal world that would accept me. And to be honest, I probably wouldn't make a good Healer, just like I probably wouldn't last as a magical fixer, either. Not yet, anyway. I was determined to change my ways. I was going to learn to color inside the lines, and I had six months to do it.

As I ate my breakfast at the small two-person table in the corner of the room, my phone dinged. That meant my daily email had arrived, with the list of plants I needed to collect by the end of the day.

I opened the email with one hand while shoving the last bite of toast into my mouth with the other and looked over the list. I worked for Magical Pharmaceuticals, one of the largest paranormal pharmaceutical companies in the world. They made pills and potions for all kinds of ailments and needed a constant supply of fresh plants for them. That was where I—and the rest of their worldwide network of plant collectors—came in. I would spend the day collecting everything they needed, then drop it all off in town by the afternoon.

Today's list of ingredients was fairly straightforward. I needed to get seventy-five leaves of wild basil, and I knew exactly where a huge field of it grew. I needed two pounds of cedar bark—again, easy—and three dozen magic morel mushrooms. Those would be a bit tough to find this time of year, but I was fairly confident I would manage.

I finished off my breakfast, grabbed my collection bag with special compartments to keep each individual plant separated from the others, and headed off. I sent a quick text to Leda, telling her I hoped her day went well, and made my way to the edge of the forest. I knew all of the paths in the woods here in Mt. Rheanier like the back of my hand.

Mt. Rheanier was surrounded by a myriad of hiking trails in a network that spanned hundreds of miles.

Some were easy, flat trails that even small children could manage, while others were steep and technical, involving ropes and basic mountaineering skills to navigate to their summits. For the latter, however, the views were often incredible.

Personally, I used the trails to get to my plants more easily. My favorite patch of wild basil was easy to get to —all I had to do was take Lakeside Trail until it intersected with Space Oddity. Then I followed that for about a mile until I reached the top of the lookout, and the field of basil was about ten feet away, inside the woods. All in all, if I didn't dawdle, the basil portion of the day would take me under an hour.

Why was the trail called Space Oddity, you ask? Great question. The wizard who designed all the trails on the western side of the lake was an aficionado of human-world music, particularly of a man named David Bowie, and named all of the trails he built after his songs.

Fall was my favorite season. I loved everything about it—the crisp morning air; wrapping myself up in thick cardigans to keep the chill out; the deep yellows, oranges, and reds of the leaves before they fell to the ground; and, of course, pumpkin-flavored everything. After all, I was an earth coven witch. Pumpkin was practically in my blood.

I happily scrunched up my nose at the nip in the air as I made my way along Lakeside Trail, named because it ran from one end of town all the way around the far side of the lake before ending up back in the other end of town. The whole loop was just over six miles long and offered phenomenal views of the town, the mountain, and the lake the whole way. It was paved, about six feet wide, and extremely popular with everyone in town, from paranormals training for marathons to families just looking to enjoy the outdoors together.

It was still early enough in the morning that I only passed a few enthusiastic runners before reaching the intersection with Space Oddity. Taking the left onto the single-track dirt trail, I slowed my pace slightly as the trail rose up into the woods. Now, rather than being surrounded by the thigh-high grass bordering the lake, I found myself in a forest of cedars, with only the occasional beam of light making it through the thick canopy of conifers.

This was basically earth witch heaven.

About twenty minutes of slow walking later, I reached the first lookout on this trail, which was right near the patch of wild basil I needed. I took a moment to sit down on a rock on the edge of the lookout, staring over the lake and the city. The bells from the old-fashioned clock at coven headquarters chimed, their sound ringing through the valley, announcing that it was nine o'clock.

Sure, I had a job to do, but that didn't mean I couldn't take a couple of minutes to enjoy the view first. Life was for living, after all.

As the peals of the bells died away, I got up from my

spot on the rock, wondering if my knees had always hurt like this, or if I was already feeling my age when I hadn't even hit thirty yet. I looked down at my knees and gasped.

The rock I was standing on dropped away at my feet, revealing a small ledge thirty feet below. There, on that ledge, was Blaze.

His eyes were closed, and his head and neck were tilted at a strange angle. Too strange.

"Blaze!" I called out, my voice cracking. It was more out of desperation than anything. The way his neck was angled, there was no way he was still alive.

Great. What was I supposed to do? Leave him here? I had to call the local Enforcers. That also wasn't the best option. I wasn't exactly on the best terms with our Chief Enforcer. But I also couldn't just leave him here.

I glanced at my bag. Ok, so the basil wasn't getting picked today. Hopefully my boss would understand. Alerting the authorities about a dead dragon shifter trumped a few basil leaves any day of the week. Even if the authorities in question and I didn't exactly get along.

I placed the call to the general Enforcer line and got a bored-sounding shifter on the other end. After all, this was Mt. Rheanier. When it came to crime, the worst that usually happened were drunk wizards casting spells they shouldn't and overly aggressive shifters attempting to mark each other's homes.

"Mt. Rheanier Enforcers."

"I'm at the first lookout on Space Oddity, about a mile from the trailhead, and there's a dead dragon shifter. I don't know if he's fallen off the ledge, or what. At least, I'm pretty sure he's dead."

I could practically feel the shifter on the other end of the line rolling his eyes. I was just another bored witch making a prank call, he must have thought.

"I'll send someone by shortly to have a look," he said. "Don't touch anything."

From the sound of things, I had a sneaking suspicion whoever he sent wasn't going to be high up on the totem pole. I sat down and sighed, thinking I probably had a decent wait ahead of me before the Enforcers got around to checking on what they would obviously have believed to be a fake call.

As soon as I saw the wizard they sent out flying toward me, I let out a groan.

"You have *got* to be kidding me. They sent *you?*" I asked as soon as Jack Stone landed in front of me. He was tall, with sandy blond hair that always fell into his eyes. The way he brushed it aside made all the witches in town swoon. It was too bad all of their attention was wasted on Jack.

"I *am* an official Enforcer now," Jack said, puffing out his chest slightly. "I know I'm the wizarding support staff, taking care of issues that require magic, but my official title is Enforcer."

In the paranormal world, Enforcers were almost always shifters. Some places made exceptions, and Mt.

Rheanier was one of them, where one witch or wizard would be hired to take care of any tasks the Enforcers needed that required the use of magic.

"So what was the magical requirement that graced me with your presence?" I asked, crossing my arms.

"Nobody else wanted to climb up here to answer a prank call, and I'm the only one who can fly a broom," Jack said with a shrug. "By the way, what was with that, anyway? You're not usually the type to do something like that. Is this to get back at me?"

"Please. Like you're that important in my life," I said, rolling my eyes. The reality was, it was exactly the sort of thing I would do to get back at Jack, but I wasn't going to tell him that. "I'm not joking."

"Seriously?" Jack peered over the ledge, and when he turned back to me, his face was a shade paler. "Have you checked to see if he's alive?"

I shook my head. "Don't have a broom to fly down and check. I just called the Enforcers straightaway."

"Good. Stay here."

Jack flew down to the ledge and carefully checked Blaze's body for a pulse.

"He is dead, isn't he?" I called down, and Jack nodded.

"Yeah. And I don't think this was an accident."

CHAPTER 4

*J*ack immediately called for backup, and half an hour later the town's Chief Enforcer showed up. Lea Loeb had short blond hair and dark brown eyes; she was a lion shifter through and through. We'd had a couple of run-ins when I was back at the Academy as a teenager. Nothing too serious; I may have just taken a few potions that were a bit less than legal a couple of times.

She nodded at me, all professionalism, when she arrived. Despite the fact that it wasn't the easiest hike, she wasn't the least bit out of breath.

"What have we got?"

"Blaze the dragon," Jack replied. "He's on the ledge. Broken neck and leg."

"What makes you think it wasn't an accident?" Chief Enforcer Loeb asked.

"There's a knife underneath his body, and some

GOING THROUGH THE POTIONS | 23

blood. I think he was stabbed before he was pushed off the ledge."

My stomach turned. Blaze, murdered? Who on earth could have wanted to murder a dragon like him? I had known him for years, and he was a nice guy. He came from one of the richest shifter families in town, but he never flaunted his wealth. He did a bit of work here and there and volunteered for a lot of things, like taking part in Keith's testing sessions. I knew he also did quite a few things for the shifter community.

"Can you bring the body up?" Chief Enforcer Loeb asked, and Jack nodded, moving back to the ledge and pulling out his wand. The Chief Enforcer turned to me. "Can you tell me everything that happened here this morning?"

I recounted my tale, leaving nothing out. I couldn't believe Blaze had been murdered, and more than anything, I wanted to make sure the person who did this to him was found and brought to justice. I might not have been the best-behaved witch on the planet, but one thing was certain: murder was wrong, and the murder of good paranormals like Blaze was even worse.

Chief Enforcer Loeb took notes as I spoke, nodding here and there. When I finished, I took a deep breath and looked around. A couple of other Enforcers who had arrived with her were looking over the body. I couldn't help but look myself. He almost looked peaceful. Well, apart from his neck being at an almost ninety-degree angle.

My eyes drifted over to the knife lying on the ground next to him. It was plain, with a wooden handle and a blade that was maybe six inches long. A kind of multipurpose knife that was both common and virtually untraceable. It certainly wasn't one of the samurai swords that weirdo Ryan Westwood kept in his basement. That would have been way too good a clue.

"Right," Chief Enforcer Loeb eventually told me. "Thank you for your help. I'll ask you now to please head back into town. And I know this is Mt. Rheanier and nothing stays secret for long, but if you could avoid telling anyone what you saw until we have a chance to tell the family, I would appreciate it."

I nodded numbly. "I won't be telling anyone, I promise," I said. I meant it. I didn't want Blaze's family to find out about this at the local coffee shop. I started to head down the path, and Jack joined me, finding it difficult to walk next to me on the narrow path, especially when I purposely walked in the middle to deter him.

"Listen," he said. "I know you're mad at me. But we used to be friends, and I still care about you. I want to make sure you're ok."

I stopped and turned to him, my hands on my hips. "You didn't make sure I was ok when you started banging my boyfriend behind my back."

Jack winced. "I know. That was a mistake. I'm sorry.

I wish you could have found out the truth about Sean another way."

I had been dating Sean Ashton for a year when I caught him in bed with Jack—one of my best friends, of all people. I had thought we were going to get married. But hey, that's just the kind of girlfriend I was, the type that drove their boyfriends to the realization that they were, in fact, gay.

Deep down—like, *really* deep down—a part of me was happy for Sean. I was glad he was finally able to get in touch with his true feelings, and I knew in reality, our marriage wouldn't have been happy with Sean secretly pining for other wizards. But I hadn't been able to forgive either one of them for the *way* in which I found out the truth.

I had been hurt in a way I didn't know I could hurt, and I wasn't sure if I was ever going to be able to forgive them. I certainly didn't plan on it.

"Yeah, if only there was a way to tell me the truth that didn't involve seeing you both butt naked on my bed," I replied sarcastically. I kept moving down the hill, refusing to look back. Thankfully, Jack didn't follow after me.

I went straight home, lay back down on my bed, and stared at the ceiling for a while.

"*A*lthea! Althea, I know you're in there. Answer the door." I groaned and grabbed a pillow, pulling it over my head to drown out the sound of my mother, but I knew it was no use. She knew I was home, and so she was going to keep knocking until I answered.

"Coming, Mom," I whined. I must have fallen asleep eventually, because when I opened the door the sun had set. With her long black hair and black eyes, staring at my mom was like looking into the future. We looked like sisters with a twenty-five-year age gap between us. "What is it?"

"I heard about Blaze, and word is you're the one who found him. I've made some stew for dinner; come over and have a bowl. I also made some cheesecake for dessert. Your favorite."

Alright, so my mom knew the best way to my heart was through my stomach. As soon as I heard the word "stew," my mouth started watering, and she sealed the deal with the promise of cheesecake. My stomach grumbled; I hadn't actually eaten anything at all since that morning. "I'll be there in five minutes."

"Good."

I closed the door, ran a brush through my hair, and made my way up to the main house that my mom now shared with my sister and my grandma. It was small—tiny, really—but I had grown up here, and this little cottage would always hold a special place in my heart.

Especially since I knew how hard my mom had worked to keep us in this little space.

"There you are," my grandma Rosie exclaimed when she saw me. Her hair was curled and dyed an interesting apricot color. She couldn't have been taller than five feet and was surprisingly spry for a woman of her age. "I heard you saw a body today. Tell me everything."

I sighed. "I'd really rather not."

"Oh, come on, you have to. I need to know literally everything." I sat down at the small dining table while my mom shot her own mother a look.

"You don't need to know everything. Just look at her, Mother. Ali's obviously had quite the shock, and you should leave her alone to eat her stew."

My mom glared at Grandma Rosie as she placed a heaping bowl of beef stew laden with tender pieces of meat and thick chunks of vegetables in front of me. The aroma of rosemary and thyme rose to my nostrils and I grabbed the thick chunk of bread next to the bowl and chowed down before Grandma Rosie could keep harassing me.

"You're going to have to stop eating eventually," Grandma Rosie said.

"Why do you care so much, anyway?" I asked through a giant mouthful of stew. "You're not usually so macabre."

"Althea, don't talk with your mouth open, you're almost thirty," my mom scolded from her spot in front of the oven.

"Haven't you heard?" Grandma Rosie replied. "Blaze's family have put up a reward to whoever can find the killer. Half a million abras."

I raised my eyebrows. "Half a million? Seriously?"

"That's right. Connie Sutherland told me about it this afternoon, and we've decided we're going to work together to find the killer. That's why I need to know everything. Having access to the person who found the body is our secret weapon."

I looked at Grandma Rosie suspiciously. "How did you find out I was the one who found the body, anyway?"

"Oh, everyone knows that," Grandma Rosie said, waving away my question. Mom brought over a couple more bowls of stew and sat down at the table with the two of us. "It was all over town. So, what was it? Stabbed in the heart? Was there blood everywhere?"

"Is this really a conversation you want to be having at the dinner table?" Mom asked, shooting daggers at Grandma Rosie.

"Oh, don't be so sensitive," Grandma Rosie shot back while I hid a smile. There was a reason Grandma Rosie was called Crazy Rosie by most people in town. And yet her friend Connie actually made her look normal. The two of them looking into a murder was probably not a good thing.

"He was stabbed, with a knife, and then pushed off a ledge," I explained. "That's all I'm telling you, because it's all I know."

"Well, do the Enforcers have any suspects yet?"

"How on earth should I know?"

"Weren't you eavesdropping?"

"Of course I didn't eavesdrop on the Enforcers discussing a murder."

"Well, here I thought you were the more useful of my two granddaughters. I guess I was wrong."

"Well I, for one, am *glad* that I raised a daughter who doesn't eavesdrop on the Enforcers," Mom said to Grandma Rosie.

"I'll be glad when I get that half million abra reward," came Grandma Rosie's reply.

"Is that real?" I asked.

"Of course it's real. They want their son's killer found. Of course, I saw Chief Enforcer Loeb later on and she didn't look particularly happy, but what can you do?"

"So how are you going to find the killer?" Mom asked.

"You're not going to tell me not to do it?"

"You're my mother. You're thirty years older than I am. If you're going to make bad life decisions, don't let me stop you. Just let me know if you get yourself arrested so I don't end up with too many leftovers for dinner."

"Well, that's not what a mother wants to hear from her daughter."

"No daughter wants to hear that her mother has

decided to become a private investigator as a septuage-narian, either."

"That's ageist," Grandma Rosie replied.

I ignored the bickering and focused on my stew, but my mind kept going back to the reward money. After all, I was barely scraping by on my current salary, and I had to wait another six months to try the test to be accepted as a magical fixer again. Half a million abras would certainly get me a lot closer to buying my mom the kind of home she deserved, the kind of home where the kitchen table wasn't so small that my feet hit hers every time I shifted a tiny bit.

After all, if the money was up for grabs anyway, why shouldn't I be the one to get it?

CHAPTER 5

*L*eaving my mom's house satisfied and feeling like I was pregnant with twins after a bowl of stew and two slices of cheesecake, I staggered back to the shed, ready to collapse in a food coma, but thought I'd check my email first. There was a message from my boss, and I let out a groan. With the stress of the day, I'd forgotten to let him know I wasn't going to be able to make the day's deliveries.

The email told me to meet him at the company headquarters in Spokurse the following morning. Great. That was just what I needed.

Still, it was my fault for not sending out the email in the first place. I'd explain what had happened in the morning, and everything would be fine. And then I'd come home and sneak another slice of that delicious cheesecake.

At least, that was the plan. Reality had a different idea.

I woke up the next day, got dressed, and stopped by my favorite local coffee shop, The Magic Brewmstick. They had an absolutely perfect location, right on the lake. The entrance was marked with a swinging wooden sign that hung above the door, and once I stepped inside, I was immediately blasted with the aroma of roasted coffee beans. The ceiling was low, with dark exposed beams throughout the space and industrial-style lighting. It certainly wasn't meant to be bright and airy. However, once I received the coffee I had ordered, I stepped out onto the patio on the other side and found myself in a perfect oasis here in the center of town. My feet were nestled in lush grass, surrounded by picnic tables that gave a perfect view over the lake. Strings of fairy lights hung around the tall wooden fence that enclosed either side of the patio, allowing for a bit of privacy.

Yes, this was the perfect way to spend a few minutes in the morning. Even the coolest witches like myself were allowed to enjoy a calm fall morning.

Of course, my personality meant that I was able to enjoy myself for exactly five minutes before I started getting impatient. I finished off my coffee, brought the mug back inside, and headed toward the portal to Spokurse.

The Magical Pharmaceuticals headquarters was in a huge steel and glass building right in downtown

Spokurse. Walking through the front doors felt eerily like passing through the jaws of a futuristic monster. I walked past the shifter guards in the lobby and made my way up to the fourth floor, where the elf Florondir, who was in charge of all the company's plant collectors, had his office.

Now, personally, I had always thought elves were super creepy. That whole thing where they can sense another paranormal's feelings? That's so far over the line of creepy, it belongs in the plot of a horror movie, not real life. And of all the creepy elves in the world, Florondir took the cake. For one thing, there was the way he decorated his office. In the sense that there *were* no decorations. And when I say no decorations, I don't mean that he skipped the potted plant in the corner. I mean I walked into his office and looked at four completely blank walls painted pure white, without a single photo hanging on them. The floor and ceiling were also white, and the room's furniture consisted entirely of a white desk, behind which Florondir sat, and a white chair on the other side of the desk that I immediately sank into, trying to ignore the fact that this office gave me the heebie-jeebies. Seriously, this was the sort of place a serial killer would use as his office. Was it soundproof? I bet it was soundproof.

I forced the thought out of my head and tried to convince myself that I was going to make it out of here alive. Florondir was tapping away at his computer, which was, you guessed it, a white Mac. Goodness.

How long was this going to take? I wanted to get my day's assignment and get out of here.

Florondir's eyes moved from his screen to my face. His eyes were blue like the glacier ice on Mt. Rheanier in the summer. Again, super creepy.

"A little impatient this morning?" he asked. "My apologies. I will be only a moment longer."

There it was again, that super creepy habit of sensing people's feelings. "Take your time, I'm fine," I said, plastering a smile on my face that I hoped looked genuine.

Two minutes later, Florondir looked away from his screen. "Do you know why I've called you in today?"

"Because I forgot to send you an email yesterday telling you why I didn't bring in my plants."

"That's right," Florondir nodded. "Do you have an explanation for me?"

"I do," I said. "I came across the body of a murdered friend near the field I collect wild basil from, so after I called the Enforcers and they took over, I decided to go home and take the rest of the day." Ok, calling Blaze a friend was a bit of a stretch. He was more of an acquaintance, but I figured the white lie would only help my cause.

"Was the body in the basil field?"

"No, over a ledge nearby."

"So there was no reason why you couldn't have collected the basil after speaking with the Enforcers?"

"Other than the fact that I'm not a psychopath?"

Sometimes my mouth worked faster than my brain. It wasn't my fault; I couldn't help it.

Florondir's lips tightened. "I don't understand why you didn't simply do your work afterward."

"Well, I don't know how many times you've come across your friends' dead bodies, but this was a first for me, and I wasn't exactly in the right headspace to do anything. I'm sorry I didn't email you. The fact that I didn't think of it should give you a good idea of how I was doing, mentally. Besides, the Enforcers told me to get out of the area. I don't think they would have let me collect the basil regardless."

"The fact is, here at Magical Pharmaceuticals, your contract is clear: in the case of a close family member's death, you are allowed two days off for mourning. This death was that of a friend, not a family member, and therefore you are in breach of your contract, and we are terminating your employment."

The words hit me like a pile of bricks over my head. "Wait, what?"

"You were unable to bring the herbs required in time, as you are required to do, and we cannot have plant collectors on staff who decide to take days off whenever they face a minor inconvenience. You will be paid for all of your work up until yesterday."

"A minor inconvenience? You call stumbling across a dead body a minor inconvenience?" Rage rose up inside of me. I couldn't believe I was being fired. What on earth?

"Yes. It does not fall under your contract stipulations that justify taking an unexpected day off."

"You're joking. I already told you, regardless of that fact, the Enforcers wouldn't have let me get to the basil anyway. And I would have had to continue along the path that they had closed to get to the other two spots I needed. So no, I couldn't have gotten the plants yesterday no matter what."

"You're a witch; you could have flown there. Was there nowhere else you could have gotten the wild basil from?"

"I don't know of another patch large enough for what I had to get yesterday."

"Well, perhaps you should learn the area better. The fact is, you didn't bring us the plants, and so we're firing you."

I stood up and stormed out of the creepy office. As I left the big steel and glass building, I wiped angry tears from my eyes. I was pissed. How dare they fire me for this? I had worked for the company for a few years now, and I had always, *always* gotten them their herbs. Now, this one time I messed up because I found a body in the forest and needed to take a bit of a break to recover, they fired me?

No, this was bull. Total bull.

I looked up at the headquarters when I got about a hundred yards away, rage filling my body. I couldn't believe I'd been fired for that. One day. *One day* of not doing exactly what they wanted, and I'd been fired.

Heck, I wouldn't have been able to collect the plants even if I had wanted to. I wouldn't have been able to get enough basil from the other spots.

I pulled out my wand and pointed it directly at the windows at around the height of Florondir's office. *"Rhea, goddess mother, paint this building and make it permanent."*

A giant glob of paint flew out from my wand and splattered the windows two or three stories up. Thanks to my spell, it would be especially difficult for anybody to remove that paint. I grinned to myself, pleased with my petty act of revenge, and ran off toward the portal before any shifters arrived, looking to bring me to justice for what I'd done.

CHAPTER 6

The reality was, I didn't feel any better after having vandalized my former employer's building. After all, I still now faced the same problem: I had absolutely no income, and no future prospects. I walked around town, avoiding home. I didn't want to run into my mother by accident and have to explain to her how her screwup daughter managed to get fired from one of the lowest-paying and easiest jobs in the paranormal world.

I needed a way to get some more money, and fast. That was when the conversation with Grandma Rosie from last night came back to me. Was Blaze's family really offering half a million abras to whoever solved his murder? I needed to find out for sure.

I sent a text to my best friend, Willow. How on earth we had ever become good friends was absolutely beyond me. Willow was the complete opposite of me in every single way. She had always studied hard, and while she wasn't a particularly talented witch, thanks to her willingness to do everything it took when we were at the Academy, she now worked as a Healer and made good money doing it. She was the kindest witch I had ever known, although she was quite shy. That was how we had met: in the Academy, when we were about fourteen years old, a few of the "cool" wizards had decided they could take advantage of her, thinking that because Willow didn't have a big group of friends and kept to herself, they would be able to bully her into doing their work for them.

I found them having cornered Willow behind coven headquarters one day, with her begging them to leave her alone. When they wouldn't, I stepped in and, with a few carefully cast spells, managed to drive them away. To this day, I don't think Michael Redwood's mother knows why he had come home that day with his skin turned blue and his hands and feet shrunk to the size of tennis balls.

What can I say? I was pretty creative as a child.

Ever since that day, Willow and I had been insepa-rable. It turned out her need to work hard and be successful the traditional way meshed well with my ambition that took a slightly different form, although at the moment it looked like hers was a lot more successful. After all, I was about to beg her to pay for my coffee because I couldn't afford it.

Willow suggested we meet for lunch instead,

insisting in the text that she treat me, and at the same time as I was filled with shame for not being able to even afford to buy myself lunch at a local restaurant, I was also filled with gratitude at my friend who understood my situation and never made me feel bad for it.

We agreed to meet at a small café a few blocks away from the lake, and by the time I got there ten minutes later, Willow was already sitting at one of the tables, waving at me. Willow Desrochers was short, just a couple inches over five feet, with a medium build and a heart-shaped face. Her chestnut hair reached halfway down her back, but it was always tied back in a ponytail. Her blue eyes lit up as soon as they saw me, and I made my way over to her, giving her a quick hug.

"Thanks so much," I said. "For everything."

"No problem. I hope you don't mind that I ordered for you."

I grinned. Every time we went to this café, I always ordered the same thing: broccoli and cheese soup, half a club sandwich, and a root beer. At this point, Willow definitely knew my order off by heart.

"Only if you got me the usual," I said, sitting at the table across from her. The café here had a real rustic barnyard feel to it. The chairs and tables were made of wood that had been painted white, with a few rustic streaks still visible in the paint. It was a light and airy space, with high ceilings and light hardwood floors. Even the brick walls had been painted white, and the windows at the front went from the floor to the ceiling, allowing as much light as possible to flow in. This was the perfect spot for a beautiful early fall lunch.

"I heard you were the one who found Blaze," Willow said quietly after I had sat down. I nodded glumly.

"Yeah, that was me," I said, recounting the previous day's events. Willow shook her head sadly.

"Such a shame. He was nice. Whenever we needed a dragon to volunteer to show the Healer trainees some dragon-specific stuff, he was always willing to come by and let the trainees poke and prod him."

"He was nice. Even though he didn't go easy on me in the test to become a magical fixer."

"How did that go?" Willow asked, and I recounted the entire sorry tale to her, with her face falling when she realized I wasn't going to be allowed into the training.

"That sucks! I'm sorry, Ali. But hey, at least you know for next time that you not only have to get the collar off, but you have to do it without potentially burning down the entire town in the process."

"Technically it was Blaze that was burning down the whole town," I said with a grin. "You're right, though. I want to sit here and be angry at Keith for failing me and say that because I got the collar and there were no extra conditions, I should have passed, and a part of me does still think that, but at least in six months I'll know better."

"He is right, though," Willow said. "I know you

don't want to hear it, but when you're a magical fixer, you have to be a scalpel. You have to carefully figure out what the problem is and surgically fix it without destroying anything else around it. You're more of a hammer. You'll get the job done, but you'll also go through and wreck everything in your path doing it. I think the best thing for you to work on is your subtlety and your finesse."

"Please, I've got finesse up to here," I said, shooting Willow a rude gesture, and she laughed.

"Evidently, you were just little miss subtlety."

I was luckily saved from having to come up with a clever comeback by the arrival of our food. Willow and I spent a couple of minutes digging into our meals, and when my sandwich was half eaten and my soup bowl empty, I looked at Willow and told her the news I was so ashamed of that I'd avoided it so far.

"I got fired from my job," I told her. Her fork, holding a meatball and a couple of pieces of penne, stopped halfway to her mouth.

"What? Are you serious?"

I nodded, staring down into my empty bowl. "Yesterday, I didn't get my herbs. After I found Blaze's body, the Enforcers sent me away, and I ended up just going home and sleeping all day. I wouldn't have been able to get them anyway—there wasn't enough basil outside of the giant patch, and with the Enforcers there, I wouldn't have been allowed in the area. Florondir called me in this morning and fired me."

"For *one day* of not getting your herbs? And when you couldn't, because of the body?"

I nodded glumly. "Yup. That's all it took."

"That's ridiculous," Willow said, obviously outraged on my behalf. "Is there anything you can do?"

"Well, I vandalized the building on my way out."

"Is there anything *legal* you can do?" Willow said, shooting me a disapproving glance. "Can you appeal, or anything like that?"

"I'm not sure, but I don't think so. Normally I wouldn't care. After all, it's not like being a plant collector is prestigious, and it certainly doesn't pay well. But now that I have to wait six months before I can train to be a magical fixer, I just don't really have a lot of options."

Willow's face fell. "I'll see if the hospital is hiring any witches and wizards right now. There might be something in maintenance. It wouldn't pay well, but at least you would be able to get by."

"Thanks," I said with a small smile. "Have you heard anything about Blaze's family offering a reward to whoever can find his killer?"

"Sure," Willow said. "It's all anybody was talking about at the hospital this morning. Half a million abras to whoever can find the killer and make sure they're convicted of murder."

"Grandma Rosie was talking about it last night, too. She and Connie have decided they're going to try and solve the crime."

Willow groaned. "Yes, that's just what this town needs, the two craziest old ladies going around pretending to be super sleuths. Is your grandma even able to cast spells anymore?"

"With varying levels of success," I replied with a smile, my mind turning back to a couple of weeks earlier. Grandma Rosie had tried to cast a spell that would make a wooden spoon stir her tomato sauce automatically, but instead, the spoon began flicking the sauce all around the kitchen, hurling globs of hot tomato at the walls, windows, ceiling, and floors.

When Mom had come home, she had thought an intruder had slaughtered her mother, and Grandma Rosie was henceforth banned from ever casting spells inside my mother's kitchen again.

"Well, hopefully Chief Enforcer Loeb can get to the bottom of this before your grandmother and her best friend create even more chaos while trying to solve this crime."

"I was actually thinking that I might try and solve it," I suggested quietly, not entirely sure how Willow was going to react.

"You?" she asked, raising an eyebrow.

"Yeah, me," I said. "Think about it. I don't have a job right now, so I have plenty of time on my hands. And you say I need to practice being a scalpel rather than a hammer. What better way to practice subtly solving puzzles than by trying to solve this puzzle in particular? After all, what a magical fixer does isn't really all that different from trying to solve a murder."

"Other than the part where doing this would end up with you being in the crosshairs of a killer," Willow said, crossing her arms. "For you, it might be a puzzle, but for the murderer, it's about getting away with it. If you manage to get close, you're probably going to end up in his sights."

"Not if I do it subtly," I said with a smile and a wag of my finger. "I can figure out who it is, go to Chief Enforcer Loeb, and give her all of the information, and she can deal with the actual confrontation while I get paid the money."

Willow still looked skeptical. "I don't know," she said. "It still seems pretty dangerous to me."

"Well, for half a million abras, I'm willing to put myself in harm's way."

"It's not even guaranteed money," Willow said. "You only get paid if you actually manage to find the killer."

"Yeah, and if I don't succeed, the killer would have no reason to come after me. So it only becomes dangerous if I actually deserve the money."

"That makes so little sense my brain doesn't even know how to reply to you right now," Willow said, shaking her head. "I know I'm not going to be able to dissuade you from this, since once you've got an idea in your head you always go for it, no matter how bad of an idea it is. But please, I'm begging you, be careful. This isn't you casting spells on idiot teenagers trying to bully me anymore. This is you going after somebody who legitimately murdered one of our citizens."

"I know," I said quietly. "But I promise I'll be careful. I'll be a scalpel, just like you when you're healing people."

Willow still didn't look convinced. "Well, if there's anything I can do to help that doesn't involve committing any crimes or doing anything that might get us murdered, let me know."

"Thanks," I said gratefully. "You really are the best friend I could ever ask for."

"Just do me one favor: absolutely do not do this with your grandmother and Connie, please. Those two old ladies are insane, and having them involved in this too is just not going to end well."

I laughed. "Absolutely agreed. I'm not going near either one of them with a ten-foot pole."

CHAPTER 7

*W*illow and I finished eating, with Willow catching me up on her life, and the two of us split up. She went back to work while I began walking along the lake, trying to figure out how I was going to investigate a murder.

It wasn't like I didn't know anything. One of my guilty pleasures was watching human-world police procedurals on TV; I was a big fan of a show called Hawaii Five-0, so I figured I wasn't completely lost in this space. The first thing I had to do was try and find some suspects. Who would want Blaze dead, and why?

To do that, I knew I had to speak with the people who knew him best. That meant going deep under Mount Rheanier, to the caves where the dragons spent most of their time. I had never been there, but I did know the way. Heading back into town, I took the road that led directly toward the mountain. It eventually ended and turned into yet another forest trail, and I walked along, enjoying the sounds of the late-season birds that either hadn't migrated yet or were going to brave the winter here in Washington. After about an hour of walking, I reached the base of the caves where the dragons lived. It was currently guarded by a large black and blue dragon.

As soon as he saw me, he let out a roar, then shifted back into human form.

"What brings you to the dragon's lair?" he asked. "We are in mourning and not receiving visitors."

"I'm sorry for your loss," I said genuinely. "I was hoping to speak with some of Blaze's friends. I was the one who found him on the ledge yesterday."

The dragon shifter's face softened. "I'm sorry you had to see that. Thank you for finding him. But I'm afraid I still cannot let you in there. We have had paranormal after paranormal coming in to question the family and friends of Blaze, before the funeral has even been held. I'm afraid I cannot let anybody who is not a dragon into the caves right now."

"That's alright, I understand," I said. "Can you tell me when the funeral will be?"

"It will be held tomorrow morning, exactly forty-eight hours after the discovery of the body. Normally, we do it forty-eight hours after the time of death, but as we don't have an exact time yet, we have to go with when the body was found."

I nodded. "Thank you. Would you mind if I asked you a few questions?"

"You are trying to solve the murder, are you not?"

I shrugged. "I got fired from my job. I called the Enforcers when I found Blaze's body, and as a result, I wasn't able to collect all the plants I needed. So I have a lot of time on my hands right now, and I figured I might give it a shot."

"And the money the family has put up hasn't hurt, either," the dragon said, a smile flittering on his lips. I gave an embarrassed shrug in response. "Because you are the one who found his body, I will answer whatever questions I can. But I cannot allow you into the caves."

"I understand," I replied. "Can you think of anyone who might have wanted Blaze dead?"

"Of course not. I've been thinking of nothing else since I heard the news. Blaze was a good dragon. He was very helpful in the community, and always willing to help out when someone had an emergency at work and needed another shifter to take over."

That made sense. Shifters worked almost exclusively in roles of security or law enforcement. A lot of the dragons in town who worked security required very little training, and so it would have been possible for Blaze to cover a shift easily.

"Had he been having any issues with anyone recently? Perhaps not something that would result in his death, but even a minor spat?"

The dragon thought for a minute, then nodded. "Yes, come to think of it, I think there was something."

"Oh?"

"A few days ago, I saw him along one of the paths. He was in the middle of a heated discussion with one of the wizards from your coven; I believe his name is Jason."

"Jason Oakland?"

"Short, with black hair, and beady eyes? Looks a little bit like a rat?"

"Yeah, that's Jason Oakland," I nodded. "What were they arguing about?"

"I'm not sure. I didn't want to intrude, of course, so when I saw their conversation was very private, I moved on. But I did hear Blaze telling Jason that he needed to stop, and that was final. Jason told Blaze that he didn't know what he was talking about, and that if Blaze didn't get off his back, he'd be sorry. That's all I know."

"Ok, thanks," I said, nodding slowly. I had never liked Jason, and I wondered what Blaze had to do with him. Jason was a few years older than me, maybe six or seven years older, and even when I was growing up, he had a reputation of being a loser. I had no idea what he did for money, but I was fairly certain he didn't have a real job. "Do you know when Blaze disappeared? When was the last time anyone saw him?"

"Late the night before he was killed," the dragon replied sadly. "He ate dinner with his family, then apparently he received a text message around eleven and said he was going out. He never came back."

So that meant he could have been killed any time between eleven at night and around maybe ten the next morning, when I found the body.

"Alright, thanks," I said to the dragon. "I'll see you at the funeral tomorrow. I'm sorry again for your loss."

"Thank you," the dragon replied. "I do hope the reward offered by the family results in a quick resolution."

So did I. Hopefully a resolution that would lead to me having enough money to tide me over for a little while.

I walked back to town with my hands buried in my pockets, deep in thought, staring at the ground in front of me. That was a long window during which it was possible Blaze was killed. I wondered if maybe the Enforcers didn't have a more definite time of death, now that they would have had the body examined by Healers. I also wanted to know what the text he received that had him leave the house late at night was.

Unfortunately, I didn't think there was much of a way for me to find out either one of those things. The information would be at the town hall, protected by shifters. I could always try and break in, but no, that would probably land me in a lot more hot water than I was after right now.

Still, I was stuck. I figured at the funeral the next day I could get some more information, so I made my way back home and spent the afternoon chilling out, enjoying my first afternoon of unemployment in years.

*T*he next morning, Leda and I decided to go to the funeral together.

Leda and Willow were actually quite similar in a lot of ways. Maybe that was why I got along with Willow so well, and why I had stopped to help her back at the Academy when the wizards were bothering her. Neither witch was particularly skilled, but they both worked hard to get good grades. Leda had graduated from the Academy a couple of years ago and worked for a small, local manufacturing company making magical bath bombs, shampoos, soaps, and other health and beauty products.

Leda and I had the same black hair as our mother, but her face was rounder, her mouth thinner, taking more after our father. Leda lived in a studio apartment in town; being as she made a better living than I did, despite being the younger sibling, she could afford to move out, unlike myself, who lived in the shed at the back of the cottage.

"How are you doing?" Leda asked when I met her on the street in front of her apartment. The two of us were dressed in dark blue, the traditional color for a dragon funeral in Mt. Rheanier.

I shrugged. "I'm ok, thanks. I'm always ok."

"I'm not sure that's true," Leda said, looking at me askance. "I heard you lost your job as a plant collector."

I sighed. "Seriously? Is that news making its way around town already?" It figured. Weren't small towns always that way?

"Does Mom know yet?"

"I don't think so. She hasn't knocked down the front door in an attempt to yell at me for messing up my life."

"Do you want to talk about it?"

"Not even a little."

Leda and I walked along in silence for a few minutes. "How are you doing?" I finally asked her. "Is everything ok at work?"

"It's great," Leda said cheerily. "I'm really happy with how things are going. I came up with a cool new recipe the other day. It's a bath bomb that makes you hallucinate so you feel like you're swimming in the tropics."

"Oh, that sounds cool."

"I'll bring you one to try out. It took me ages to get the potion right. One of my first attempts failed so miserably I thought I was swimming through the River Styx, and when I finally came to, I had splashed water all over the bathroom." Leda laughed. "But I got there in the end. It just took a few attempts, and at least now I know how to make a bath bomb for my enemies."

That was my sister, always looking on the bright side of everything.

The funeral was to take place at the top of Mt. Rheanier. Someone had created a series of magical gondolas that went from the trail leading to the dragon caves all the way up to the location of the funeral. The gondolas were large, each holding eight or so paranormals comfortably, and moved up and down the mountain, gliding wirelessly a few feet above the trees. Leda and I stepped into one together and were immediately whisked up, with my sister pressed against the window, enjoying the view.

"I do think I should make the time to go to the top of the mountain more," she said to me. "I just wish there was a way to do it without flying. They should make this gondola a permanent installation."

"Yeah, but then what? You'd get to the top and you'd just freeze in the wind and cold until you couldn't stand it anymore, and you'd come back down."

"Sure, but someone could build a large building up there to hold visitors. The view is fantastic. I mean, look at that."

Leda had a point about the view. Looking out of the gondola as we rose above the entire mountain was absolutely amazing. The whole valley spread out below us. The sun's rays glanced off the calm waters of the lake, with the town's adorable buildings so small they looked like toys. The leaves on the deciduous trees were turning, mingling with the deep pine color of the evergreens.

We reached the top of the mountain and stepped

out. I immediately wrapped my arms around myself; it was significantly colder at the higher elevation, and the wind was not only cutting, but it was also a lot stronger. My hair whipped around my face as I looked around.

We were standing on a large ledge at the top of the mountain, giving us a 360-degree view of the world around us. To the left was the large caldera of Mt. Rheanier, about a hundred feet deep and maybe three hundred feet wide, and almost a perfect circle. Paranormals were streaming toward it, and Leda and I joined the crowd, following a path deep into the crater formed by the last explosion of this mountain some thousands of years ago. As we stepped down into the hole, the wind abated, but it was still significantly colder than in the valley below.

In the center of the caldera was a huge bonfire. Leda and I approached it, joining the group of paranormals who all streamed toward the fire, everyone pretending that wasn't at all for its warmth.

I looked around to see if I recognized anyone before the funeral ceremony began. After all, I wasn't here just to mourn Blaze—I was here to see if I could find his killer.

CHAPTER 8

$\mathcal{M}$y eyes scanned the crowd. It seemed as though half of Mt. Rheanier had come to pay their respects to Blaze. On the other side of the fire was a group of dragons huddled in a circle. Standing away from them, her arms wrapped around herself, tears streaming down her face, was a dragon shifter I recognized as Blaze's sister, Bridget. She had always been nice, and my heart broke for her as I saw her standing there by herself. I made my way toward her.

"Hey," I said softly to her as I approached. She still jumped a bit, as if I'd surprised her.

"Althea, right?" she said by way of greeting. "You're the one who found my brother."

"That's right," I said with a nod. "I'm sorry for your loss."

"Thank you. I can't believe anyone would do this to him. Who would have wanted him dead?"

"I was hoping you would be able to help me with that."

Bridget turned and gave me a hard look. "Let me guess, you're after the reward money."

"I'm not going to lie to you. I am," I said, holding my arms out. "I lost my job, and so I have nothing better to do than try and solve your brother's murder. To be honest, though, I liked Blaze. He was nice. I don't think he deserved what happened to him, and as much as the money would be nice, I also think the more people helping to find his killer, the better."

"You really think that, do you?"

I raised an eyebrow. "You don't agree? But it's your family that's put up the reward money."

"My mom and dad put up the reward money," Bridget stated. "I told them it was a bad idea. Do you know how many people have come by the caves looking for information? Everyone and their familiar is trying to solve this case."

"I'm sorry," I said, a bit of guilt washing over me. "I didn't mean to intrude."

"No, I understand. Really, I do. And of everyone, you're the one who found him. So I thank you for it."

"I understand he left the house the previous night and didn't come back?"

"That's right," Bridget sighed. "We were playing

cards, and he got a text, and he left. I don't know where he went, I don't know who the text was from. All I know is that it was there. And I don't know who would have wanted to kill him. You knew Blaze. He was so friendly, and he got along with everyone."

"I know," I said quietly. "I've been having trouble understanding who might have wanted to do this to him, too."

"He had been trying to find himself recently," Bridget said sadly. "It wasn't easy for him. Our family has so much money, he didn't want to take a job away from somebody who might have needed it, but he also didn't want to spend his life just sitting around doing nothing. He wanted to make something of himself, you know?"

I nodded. "I can understand that. He was a good dragon, but he definitely had a lot of energy, and I can see how a life of simple luxury would have not been for him. He seemed like the type who wanted to do more."

"That's right," Bridget said. "He hadn't quite found what he was after. Hopefully he manages to find it in the next life."

Just then, the sky was covered as four dragons flew in a circle, slowly making their way down toward the caldera. The funeral was starting. I left Bridget and made my way back to Leda, who was standing with the other witches and wizards who had come to the funeral.

We watched as the dragons continued to spiral

toward us before eventually landing next to the bonfire, one facing east, one facing west, one facing north, and one facing south. The four dragons shot fire into the sky, and as soon as that was finished a dragon shifter in human form, standing on top of the caldera's rim, began to speak. His voice had to have been magically enhanced, as it boomed across the entire space.

"Paranormals, I thank you all for coming to remember the life of Blaze, a young dragon whose life was cut short too early. I have known Blaze since he was a hatchling, and while he may not have lived a long life, the life that he lived mattered."

The dragon continued, listing off the achievements Blaze had managed and explaining all of the volunteer work Blaze had done. When the dragon was finished, he invited anybody who so wished to come up and speak on behalf of the dead.

The first to speak was his sister, who broke down after about thirty seconds and had to be helped off the rim of the caldera. A couple of other dragons went up and spoke afterward, and I made note of their names, thinking that possibly I should try and talk to them as I worked to solve this case.

Finally, the last to speak were Blaze's parents. His mother trembled as she stood on the caldera rim, looking down at everybody.

"I want to thank each and every one of you who has come to remember the life of my little dragon. He was absolutely wonderful, and I'm so glad that even though his life was cut short, in the time that he did have with us, he was able to make such an impact on people's lives. I also know that most of you are aware, but in case you aren't, our family has put up a reward. Whoever is able to find our son's killer will be given five hundred thousand abras from us. We want the person who did this to be brought to justice. But until then, please, let us celebrate the life of the best son a mother could ever ask for."

Blaze's mother broke down then, and his father guided her off the rim of the caldera and back down toward the crowd as the dragon who had done most of the eulogy returned to the same spot.

"It is time," he announced solemnly. "Please, bring the coffin holding Blaze's body."

The four dragons standing on either side of the bonfire flew up into the air suddenly and disappeared. They returned a moment later, and this time, one of them had a plain wooden box in between his claws. The four dragons flew in a circle above the fire, and the shifter spoke once more.

"Deliver this dragon's body to the flames, allow his earthly remains to disappear as he moves into the next world."

As soon as he finished speaking, the dragon holding the box dropped it into the center of the bonfire. As soon as the box hit the flames, they exploded into a cacophony of fireworks. Blue, green, red, gold, and other colors exploded upward from the flames, the crowd gasping in a mixture of surprise and fear. The embers went out before they hit anybody, though, and instead it simply created an incredible light show as Blaze's body was incinerated by the flames.

A lump formed in my throat as the realization that I was never going to see him again really hit me. Leda took my hand and squeezed, with me returning the action back at her.

The crowd was silent, and after a couple of minutes the fireworks dissipated, the body having been taken by the flames. The four dragons shot fire into the air before flying off.

"The body of Blaze has been taken by the flames as his soul lives on in the afterlife," the dragon on the rim announced. "Thank you all for coming to the ceremony."

And with that, it was all over. Everyone began to shift and talk amongst themselves, all heading back toward the gondolas.

"Let's wait here for a while," my sister said. "After all, down here, there's no wind. Everyone is rushing to get back to those gondolas into town, which means there will be a long line in the windy cold."

"Good thinking," I said to her, my eyes scanning the crowd. Suddenly, my eyes landed on a face I recognized, and I made my way over to Jason, wanting to know exactly what he had been arguing about with Blaze before he was killed.

"Jason!" I called out. He turned and looked at me, a creepy smile growing on his face.

"Hey, you're Ali, right?"

"That's me," I replied. "I heard you got into an argument with Blaze a few days before he was killed."

The creepy smile suddenly turned a lot more hostile as Jason crossed his arms in front of him. "Oh yeah? Who told you that?"

"Doesn't matter. Is it true, or not? Did you have a fight with Blaze just before he was killed?"

"I don't need to answer you."

"Sure, you don't, but ignoring my questions definitely doesn't make you look guilty as sin. I'm sure the Chief Enforcer would love to know what I know."

Jason's eyes darted from side to side, and he really did look like a rat trapped in a cage. "Fine. Yeah, we had a little bit of a fight. But it was nothing. And I sure didn't kill the guy."

"What was the fight about?"

Jason grimaced, as if he didn't want to tell me.

"Look, you can tell me, or I can go straight to Chief Enforcer Loeb. Personally, I know who I'd rather deal with. The one who can't lock you up in jail for murder."

"I'm telling you, I didn't kill him."

"Help me believe you. What's a scumbag like you doing dealing with a good dragon like Blaze?"

"It's his sister," Jason finally admitted. "She's a fan of some...stuff that I sell on the side, and Blaze found out about it. He didn't want me selling to her anymore, and I told him it wasn't any of his business, that his sister is a grown dragon and she can do what she wants."

"And let me guess, this stuff you are selling Bridget on the side, it's some potions that aren't exactly on the legal side of things, are they?"

"Hey, what can I say? They make people feel good, and who is the wizarding body to decide what potions people can and can't enjoy?"

I resisted the urge to roll my eyes. The fact was, there was a zero percent chance that I would ever put anything in my body that Jason had created.

"Ok, so how did the fight between the two of you end?"

Jason shrugged. "I don't know. We sorted it out like two grown men with mutual respect for one another and both left happy."

"He threatened to kick your butt if you didn't stop selling to his sister and you ran off like a scared little baby, didn't you?" I asked, and as Jason shifted his weight from foot to foot, looking at the ground, I knew my guess was a lot closer to the truth. "Alright, tell me this. Where were you the night before and the morning that Blaze was killed?"

"Home. Sleeping."

"Until ten in the morning?" I raised an eyebrow.

"Look, I'm not a morning person, ok?"

"Fine, can anyone confirm that you were there?"

"I do alright with the ladies, as I'm sure you can

guess, but I'm kind of in between girlfriends right now."

"So you were by yourself."

Jason shrugged. "What can I say? One of my socks can confirm my story, since I don't have a witch in my life right now."

I scrunched my nose, not bothering to hide my disgust with Jason.

"Fine, go away," I told him. I felt like I was going to need a shower as soon as I got back into town.

Jason scampered off and I made my way back toward my sister, lost in thought.

"Everything ok?" Leda asked as I made my way toward her. I nodded.

"Yeah, sorry, I just had to ask Jason a few questions."

My sister scrunched up her nose. "I hope he did it," she said. "I know you're not supposed to think that about anybody, but frankly, since *somebody* had to kill Blaze, I'd rather it be somebody like that who nobody would miss if they went to prison. Did you know he's been selling illegal potions to people? And they're actually buying them?"

"I didn't know, but I do now," I said darkly, making a mental note to ask Willow if she knew anything about it. Being a Healer, Willow often knew about this sort of thing, because whenever anybody had an adverse reaction to potions, they invariably ended up in the hospital with her. Jason was way too terrible a wizard to manage to make illegal potions without messing up at least a few batches. I was sure of that.

The fact that Bridget had been one of his clients, however, was a surprise. I could definitely believe Blaze's reaction if he'd found out about it. Jason was a scumbag who was breaking the law, definitely. But was he a murderer? I wasn't quite so certain about that.

CHAPTER 9

*B*y the time we got back into town about an hour later, I was a little bit stuck. I really needed access to Blaze's phone to find out exactly what he had gone to do the night before. Unfortunately, I figured the phone was with the Enforcers, and there was going to be no way to get access to it.

I also quickly found out that I had bigger issues to deal with. I had turned my phone to silent during the funeral out of respect, and when Leda and I stepped into the gondola to go down, I groaned as I pulled out my phone and looked at the screen.

"What is it?" my sister asked.

"I think Mom found out I lost my job," I said with a wry smile. I had thirty-two missed calls and four text messages.

Did you seriously lose your job?

You need to come and see me right now.

I can't believe even being a plant collector was too much for you.

How on earth do you manage to lose the easiest job on the planet?

"Oh no," Leda said, frowning in sympathy. "Do you want me to come home with you when you have to face her?"

I shook my head. "No, thanks. I think I'll just get this over with."

I closed my eyes and leaned my head back against the gondola glass, trying to get rid of the wave of guilt that washed over me. It wasn't that I *tried* to be a bad daughter, or a complete failure. It was just that a lot of the time my mouth said things that were probably best left unsaid, or I acted impulsively in a way that sometimes got me into a little bit of trouble. I genuinely wanted to be more like Willow or my sister. I wished I could be the type of person who always followed the rules, who always did exactly what they were supposed to do, and who never got into the least bit of trouble.

Unfortunately, that just wasn't my reality.

When the two of us reached the valley again, I said goodbye to my sister and decided to head home, figuring that getting this conversation over and done with was the best course of action.

As soon as I stepped through the front door, my mother was there, waiting, her arms crossed in front of her.

"How long have you been standing there like that

waiting for me?" I couldn't help but ask. Perhaps not the best way to start off this conversation.

"Are you too good to answer phone calls from your mother, now?"

"I was at the funeral," I explained. "I had my phone on silent. Where's Grandma Rosie?"

"Out with Connie trying to solve that murder," Mom replied. "Now, what's this I hear about you losing your job as a plant collector, and how come you didn't tell me yourself and I had to find out from Antonia down at the bakery?"

I winced. Antonia was the town's biggest gossip, and she thrived on having information at her disposal that could embarrass others. She would have loved announcing to my mother that I was back among the ranks of the unemployed in front of everybody.

"Sorry," I muttered. "I was embarrassed."

"Not nearly as embarrassed as I was, having that fact announced in front of everybody while I was just trying to buy some bread. How did you manage to lose the easiest job in the paranormal world?"

"Because of Blaze's death, I couldn't get the basil they needed for the day, and so they fired me. It honestly wasn't my fault."

My mother's expression softened slightly. "Seriously? They fired you just for that?"

I nodded and bit back tears. "Yeah. That was all it took. I know it was a dumb job, I know it paid a pittance, and I know that I shouldn't have lost it. But there was honestly nothing I could do."

"Well, what's done is done. What are you going to do now?"

"Willow is looking into what jobs are available at the hospital," I offered. I honestly had zero desire to take a maintenance job at the local hospital. Not only did it pay just around the same as a plant collector, but it involved using magic to clean up all sorts of bodily fluids, and that was definitely not on the list of things that interested me.

"There are always manufacturing jobs as well," Mom said. "You may have to take the portal to work every day, but at least it's something."

I nodded mutely. Honestly, magical manufacturing sounded even worse than cleaning up messes at the hospital. I knew what that entailed: standing in front of the conveyor belt and casting the same spell a thousand times a day at every item that passed by. I'd probably kill myself from boredom after the first two hours.

Still, I knew better than to tell my mother that I was following in Grandma Rosie's footsteps and trying to solve the murder. I knew how she had reacted when her mother announced she was doing it; if she found out her own daughter was going to follow the same path, I could only imagine how badly she would react.

That meant I had to solve this murder quickly, before my mom started pressuring me even harder to take a manufacturing job.

"I'll look into it," I lied. "Now, if you don't mind, I was going to go into town and see if I could find a local job."

"Of course," Mom said. "If you come by around six, you're welcome to join us for dinner."

I opened my mouth to politely decline, then remembered that the only thing I had in my cupboard right now was ramen noodles. "I'll be there," I said, giving my mom a quick wave and heading back out into the street.

I had no other options. If I didn't want to live my life casting the same spell thousands of times, I was going to have to get this cash, and fast. And the only way I could do that was by solving the murder. Since I was fresh out of leads, I was just going to have to make some. I headed toward the town hall, my heart pounding in my chest.

After all, it wasn't really illegal if it was for a good cause, right?

I stared up at the large Gothic building that made up town hall. It took up an entire block by itself, with large spires reaching high into the sky. Statues of gargoyles lined the steep roof, their faces looking down at me as though mocking me in this terrible idea. The dark bricks gave it a little bit of a creepy feel, and I walked toward the front door, doing a little bit of reconnaissance.

As soon as I stepped inside, I was greeted by an Enforcer, a wolf shifter who looked at me suspiciously.

"Yes?" he asked. "What brings you to town hall this morning?"

"I need to register a business," I lied. "Third floor?"

"That's right," the shifter said, motioning to the large stone staircase in the middle of the building, leading up to the higher floors.

"Thanks," I said, flashing him a smile and making my way up the stairs. When I reached the second floor, I paused. The second floor of town hall was dedicated to the town's Enforcers, and I snuck a quick look through the window. There were six or seven shifters all sitting at their desks, with Chief Enforcer Loeb's office at the far end.

No, I definitely wasn't going to be able to make it through there unnoticed. Not even if I made it past the initial guard watching the front of the town hall.

I went up to the third floor, loitered for a while, then left, thanking the wolf shifter as I did so.

"Have a great day," he told me. I made my way back home, lost in thought. I had to find a way to get into that office. I could use an invisibility spell or potion, but because the shifters had such powerful noses, they would almost certainly sniff me out even if they couldn't see me.

I made my way into my little shed and pulled the

one book I owned down from the shelf—the big book of potions every single witch in the coven of Rhea had created. We all had one, which we started at five years old, our first year at the Academy. The book was filled with recipes for every potion we had ever come across and was added to constantly.

I flipped through the pages, trying to find a recipe for a potion that might be able to help me. Then I found one. The perfect potion, designed to mask your smell so that shifters were unable to detect your odor and make you invisible to all shifters.

My eyes scanned the recipe, checking to see how long I was going to have to wait for it to be ready. Sometimes potions could take days or even weeks before they were ready. I really hoped this one didn't fall into that category.

A smile crept onto my lips as I moved my finger down the page and settled on the time: instant. As soon as I added all of the ingredients to the pot and brought it to a boil, my potion would be ready. Perfect. Now all I had to do was find the ingredients for my potions. That wasn't going to be a problem.

I needed the following: six dried dandelion flowers, half a cup of fresh coconut milk, three hairs from a calico cat, two vials of water from melted snowfall, and eight stalks of naturally dried grass.

Luckily for me, all of those were basic ingredients every good earth coven witch had in her pantry. Of course, *I* wasn't really a good earth coven witch, but my mother and Grandma Rosie both were, so I snuck into the main house and grabbed everything I needed. I made a mental note to remind my mother to find more calico cat hairs. There were plenty of orange, black, and white, but the calico jar was getting pretty empty. I knew my neighbor had a familiar who fit the bill, but he didn't like me at the best of times, so I figured I'd leave the idea of going at his fur with a pair of scissors to my mom. I also got lucky in that she was out, so I didn't even have to lie about what it was I was making.

I snuck the ingredients back into my shed and pulled out another earth witch staple: my trusty cauldron. Made of cast iron and weighing approximately eight thousand pounds despite only being a small, one-gallon model, my mother had given this one to me on my first day of the Academy. It was traditional for all witches in our coven to receive a ceremonial cauldron from their mothers when they began their formal witch education. Many were handed down through families, and mine had once belonged to my grandmother. While I owned a few other cauldrons—some cheap brass ones, primarily—this one was my favorite and I used it at every opportunity.

I looked at the instructions and smiled. This was a very easy potion to make. I put all of the ingredients in the cauldron in order. Then I took my wand and placed it over the rim of the cauldron, facing due north. Thank goodness for my phone's compass app; it made casting spells like this way easier.

Finally, I placed my hands around the outside of the cauldron, like I was going to lift it to my mouth to have a drink, and read the words from the incantation: *"Rhea, the great goddess mother, let the earth's power make the drinker of this potion carry odor no longer."*

Immediately, the ingredients inside the cauldron were enveloped by a thick scarlet smoke that rose up, quickly filling the room. I coughed as I inhaled the smoke, which smelled like wood burning, but after about twenty seconds the smoke dissipated and I gazed into the bowl.

The mixture had turned a perfect scarlet red as well, and I tried not to think about the fact that I was going to have to drink what definitely looked a lot like blood. I preferred potions that looked more like fruit smoothies or fancy cocktails over the ones that looked like bodily fluids. So sue me.

Now I was all set. Tonight, I could go to coven headquarters, and none of the shifters on the second floor would be able to see me. I figured I'd be better off waiting until the sun went down, since Chief Enforcer Loeb would be more likely to be back home and I'd have an easier time getting access to all the information I needed.

There was absolutely no way this could go horribly wrong.

CHAPTER 10

I spent the afternoon killing some more time until finally, just after sunset, I made my way into my mother's cottage for dinner. The aroma of lemongrass and chili rose to my nostrils, and I smacked my lips in anticipation. My mom made a mean Thai green curry.

"Good, you're here. At least that makes one of you."

"Grandma Rosie still isn't back?" I asked, grabbing a large ceramic bowl from the cupboard and scooping a liberal amount of rice into it.

My mom shook her head. "I know she's my mother and that she can take care of herself, but goodness knows what kind of trouble she gets into when she's hanging around with that Connie."

I had to smile to myself; it was always funny to hear my mom complain about Grandma Rosie's friends being a bad influence. After all, the youngest of them were in their mid-sixties. The image of these sexa- and septuagenarians going around and terrorizing the town was certainly a sight to imagine.

"Well, she knows what time dinner is. If she can't be back here in time, well, she's just going to miss out," my mother muttered as she grabbed a bowl for herself. I had a sneaking suspicion my mom had repeated that same line word for word multiple times when I had been a teenager.

I ladled a thick serving of curry on top of my rice and used a fork to mush it all together into a kind of thick soup. Sitting down at the table, I took a deep breath, inhaling the delicious smells of dinner and thinking about how much better this was than sitting at home eating ramen, when the front door of the cottage burst open. I looked up to see Grandma Rosie standing there, absolutely soaking wet, dripping onto the entry mat. Her hair was plastered to her face, making her look a little bit like a wet dog that had just come out from the lake.

I was pretty sure her entire left side was covered in blue paint, too.

My mouth dropped open and stayed there.

"Well," Grandma Rosie demanded after a minute. "Are neither one of you going to get me a towel?"

My mom ran over to the bathroom and came back with a large, fluffy green towel that she handed to her mother.

"Come in, come in, and go stand near the fire. You're going to catch a cold. What on earth happened?"

"And why are you covered in paint?" I added.

"Oh, this?" Grandma Rosie asked, motioning vaguely to her left side. "This is nothing. I just had a little accident on the way out of a house."

"Oh, Rhea, mother of the gods," Mom muttered under her breath. "What on earth have you gotten yourself into? Is Connie alright? Please tell me Connie is alright. Actually, I don't want to know."

"Connie is fine, don't worry."

"Does she look like you?" I asked with a smile.

"Maybe," Grandma Rosie replied. "But the point is, I'm fine. I just need to dry off a bit. A quick spell will get rid of this paint, and then I can get some of that delicious dinner. Who knew solving crimes was such a great way to build up an appetite?"

"First you need to get some of this warming potion inside of you," my mother said, making her way to the fridge. Why on earth my mom still kept warming potion in her fridge when both her daughters were fully grown was beyond me. It was a staple among witch mothers here, a potion that immediately heats the body up from the inside to stop young witches and wizards from catching a cold when they'd been outside for too long during the winter months. I hadn't had any in years and years.

My mom brought a vial of the stuff over to Grandma

Rosie, who downed it in a single big swig. "Oh yeah, that's the stuff," she said, handing the empty vial back to my mother, who put it in the sink, shaking her head. Grandma Rosie pulled out a wand and pointed it at herself, muttering an incantation. A moment later, the paint on her side disappeared. A quick second incantation later and Grandma Rosie was back to being completely dry and looking completely normal.

Well, mostly, anyway. Her hair looked like she'd decided to take a bath with a toaster. And like she'd soaked it in bleach for a while. But apart from that, at least she wasn't dripping onto the floor anymore.

"Excellent, I love Thai food," Grandma Rosie announced, sauntering toward the kitchen and grabbing herself a plate while Mom and I looked on. She was acting like literally nothing out of the ordinary had happened at all.

"Alright, you sit down, eat some food, and tell us what on earth happened," Mom finally ordered, sitting back down in front of her bowl.

"Oh, it was nothing," Grandma Rosie said with a wave of her hand as green curry sploshed into her bowl.

"Tell us all about the nothing anyway."

"Did you know your daughter lost her job?"

Now Grandma Rosie was deflecting? How on earth was *I* the more mature of the two of us?

"I do know, and we have already discussed it. Now,

tell me what the two of you were up to, or I will go to Chief Enforcer Loeb."

"You'd really snitch to the po-po on your own mother?"

"That's right, I would," Mom replied, her arms crossed. I took another delicious mouthful of food as I watched the show, wondering who was going to hold out the longest. I was cheering for Mom; I genuinely wanted to know what Grandma Rosie had gotten herself into.

Luckily for me, the threat of being turned over to the authorities was enough for Grandma Rosie, and she muttered under her breath about how her own daughter was willing to abandon her before regaling us all with her tale.

"Now, you all know that weasel Jason Oakland?"

"Yes," I nodded. "He was seen having a fight with Blaze not long before he was killed."

"Don't tell me you're also trying to get at the reward money?" Grandma Rosie said, shooting daggers at me. I rolled my eyes and ignored her, not wanting to invite her wrath. "But yes, Althea is right. I found out he and Blaze had a fight, and I didn't know about what."

"So you went to investigate," Mom said with a sigh. "What happened?"

"Well, we didn't want to be *rude* about it. So Connie and I found out where he lived from Antonia, who we ran into at the hairdresser. Connie thought we should dye our hair to look more inconspicuous."

That explained why Grandma Rosie's hair looked like lightning streaking out of her head.

"So your idea of blending in was trying to look like Bebe Rexha," I said.

"Who?"

"Exactly," I deadpanned. "Besides, it's not like you and Connie blend in at the best of times. Literally every single person who lives here knows you. You've been staples of the town for longer than most people have been alive."

"That's why we needed to disguise ourselves. Everyone knows me as a sultry redhead. No one was expecting to see me as a blonde."

I was pretty sure "sultry" was not the first thing that came to mind when describing my grandmother.

"So you got your hair dyed, and Antonia told you all about Jason Oakland getting into a fight with Blaze, so you decided to hassle him."

"Hassle is a strong word," Grandma Rosie said. "We simply found him at work and asked him a few questions. Let me tell you, he acted *very* suspiciously. Didn't want to tell us a thing."

"Gee, I wonder why," I said, rolling my eyes once more.

"Well, after that, we thought he was our main suspect, and we wanted to go see what he was going to do. After all, we must have put the fear of Rhea into him, what with our pointed questions and his marked desire to avoid answering them."

"So you followed him," I finished.

"We did. Do you know how *boring* stakeouts can be? I thought it would be like in the movies, where you can sit in a car and enjoy copious amounts of snacks, then after a minute or two the perp comes out and you catch him in the act."

The perp? Grandma Rosie really had been watching too much television.

"So how long did it take?"

"He still had a few more hours left of his shift at work."

"I didn't realize Jason had a job right now."

"Yes, even someone like Jason Oakland managed to not join the ranks of the unemployed," Grandma Rosie said pointedly. "He works as a plant collector for Magical Pharmaceuticals. Apparently they were hiring in town."

Oh, you had to be absolutely kidding me. They fired *me* and hired *Jason Oakland* instead? Well, I supposed they reaped what they sowed. He was probably going to start planting weed in the forest so he could hide it from the Enforcers.

"So if he's working as a plant collector, how did you follow him?" Mom asked.

"Connie cast an invisibility spell on us both. We think he suspected we were there, since he kept moving around, but we were subtle."

"The two of you are about as subtle as a pair of

hippos going off a diving board," I laughed, earning myself a glare from my grandmother.

"Where did the paint come from, then?" Mom asked, wincing slightly as though she were afraid of the answer.

"I'm trying to get there, if your daughter would finish besmirching my good character."

I motioned for Grandma Rosie to continue, and she did.

"Anyway, before I was *rudely* interrupted, I was saying that the two of us snuck around, but he just seemed to go about collecting more plants. Although he did manage to confuse silverweed for white hemstail."

I was hit with the briefest feeling of satisfaction at hearing that. Silverweed and white hemstail looked quite similar, but silverweed smelled like roses when you broke a stalk of it. That was how you could tell the difference. It would figure that Jason wouldn't know that, and I hoped it ruined a whole bunch of Magical Pharmaceuticals potions when he handed them in. It would serve them right for firing me and hiring him as a replacement.

"When he was finished for the day, he went home. He lives on the first floor of one of those buildings downtown, but the problem was, his living room window is about six feet off the ground, so Connie and I couldn't see inside."

"So, of course, you didn't decide like normal people to just go home and call it a day," my mom sighed.

"Well, we'd come this far. We weren't about to give up now. What if there was blood all over his apartment? You can't make half a million abras without breaking a few laws along the way."

"There are actually a *lot* of ways to make that much money without committing felonies," my mom said with her arms crossed, glancing at me. She was obviously not particularly pleased with the life lessons her mother was teaching me.

"We didn't actually commit any crimes, unless looking through someone's window at night is a crime now." My mom buried her face in her hands as Grandma Rosie continued. "Connie went down on the ground on her hands and knees, and I was able to stand on her back and peek through the window to have a look at what Jason was doing."

"And Connie's back managed to support you?" I asked skeptically. I mean, Grandma Rosie was a tiny little thing and couldn't have weighed more than a hundred and ten pounds soaking wet, but that's still quite a bit for a woman in her mid-sixties to hold up on her back.

"Well, for a little while. We're old, not decrepit," Grandma Rosie shot at me. "Anyway, Jason moved into the other room, and he looked inside this chest he had in there. I couldn't really see it from where I was, so I adjusted my footing, and then Connie started complaining that her back hurt, and next thing I know I'm falling to the ground. There were a bunch of old cans of paint stacked up next to the house, and I tumbled into them. That's how I got the paint on me. He came out to investigate the noise so we scrambled out of there as fast as we could."

"So, basically, you spied on a guy who owns some stuff in his house," I summarized. "And you found absolutely nothing that proves he might be the killer."

"You never know," Grandma Rosie replied.

"Right," I said, hiding a smile. Well, I still liked Jason Oakland as a suspect, even if Grandma Rosie hadn't found anything that might have implicated him in the murder. I ate my soup and prepared for my own night of crime, hoping mine wasn't going to end with me covered in paint, or worse.

CHAPTER 11

*a*fter heading back to the shed feeling full and satisfied—and with a Tupperware container full of leftovers that were definitely going to be tomorrow's lunch—I measured out a vial full of the potion that I had made earlier, held my nose, and drank it.

Honestly, I had no idea if it smelled or tasted bad, but since potions tended to be a bit of a mixed bag, I never really took the risk anymore. I did my best to never smell potions if I could help it. After gulping down the mixture, which according to my book would last six hours, I didn't look or feel any different. That was one of the interesting things about potions; a lot of the time, they didn't have any noticeable effect, and you had to simply trust that you'd made them properly.

Luckily, while I was often fairly terrible at following instructions in everyday life, when it came to potions, I didn't mess around. I was fairly confident this one was made correctly and would act exactly as planned.

Unfortunately, there was no way to tell without actually running into a shifter.

I made my way casually down the dark street toward the town hall. The streets were lit with old-fashioned lamps that magically cast a warm glow on the cobbles, giving the whole town an ethereal feel. The streets were practically deserted, everyone inside for the night, and I didn't come across a single other paranormal as I made my way toward town hall.

The front door to the hall was open, and I stepped through as quietly as I could. A wolf shifter guarded the door, although rather than standing at attention, he was currently sitting on a nearby bench, stifling a yawn. I couldn't exactly blame him; the night shift had to be significantly less interesting than the day shift here.

Still, if my potion hadn't worked, he should have noticed me. Just to be sure, I waved my arms around in front of him a couple of times, but there was still no reaction. I grinned. Perfect. My potion worked. I was now invisible and scentless to all shifters, and at this time of night, there would be no one else in town hall except for the night shift Enforcers.

I made my way to the stairs and bounded lightly up them, careful not to make a sound. After all, wolf shifters had a heightened sense of hearing as well, and I didn't want to risk getting caught because I bounded around like a hippo.

Reaching the second-floor landing, I paused and looked through the hallway that led to the Enforcers' office. The door was still open, and I didn't like that. It meant that in all likelihood, there was a ward to alert someone of any intruders. I pulled out my wand.

"Rhea, mother of the gods, if this doorway is warded, allow me entry."

I whispered the incantation so as to avoid being heard by the guard below, and it worked. As soon as I finished the chant, the doorway flashed red for an instant, then changed to green. I was in.

Doing a happy dance—quietly—I snuck into the Enforcers' section of the town hall. I figured there would be no information on any of the regular desks. A murder was firmly in the "higher-ups" category of importance. So I made my way to Chief Enforcer Loeb's office, repeated my spell to kill the ward, and entered, closing the door behind me. After all, I couldn't be too careful; I didn't want the shifter down below to do the rounds, see the open door, and find me. I knew he wouldn't be able to see me, but that didn't mean I had to flaunt my presence.

I made a beeline for the desk and my eyes scanned the myriad of papers, looking for anything that might have to do with Blaze's death. They landed on a folder with the local hospital's logo, and I grabbed it, opening it and scanning the top sheet.

"Jackpot," I muttered under my breath. It was the report from the Healer who had looked at Blaze's body. I sat down at the Chief Enforcer's desk and read everything I could.

Blaze had officially died from poisoning. My eyebrows rose as soon as I read that. Seriously? I could have sworn he had been stabbed. Or, at the very least, had his neck broken. But no, the report was clear. He was poisoned, then stabbed—because it was post-mortem, that was why there was very little blood—and then his neck had been broken in the fall onto the ledge.

Someone *really* wanted to make sure they had done the job right.

But then, that meant that Blaze would have had to have drunk the potion. It had to be someone he was close to who had given it to him. After all, Blaze was in the middle of the woods when he died. No one drinks strange potions in the middle of the woods at night from someone they don't trust. That's some horror movie stuff right there.

I wondered if maybe there was a more accurate time of death, as well. After all, right now I had an approximately ten-hour window during which Blaze could have been killed. I scanned the report further. Sure enough, Blaze had been killed at eight in the morning.

Eight? Well, that was certainly strange. He had gone

out just after ten, according to Bridget and the dragon. So what did he spend the entire night doing?

The potion he had taken was listed as a very acute poison. He would have died within minutes of taking it. I recognized the type of potion. It was *extremely* advanced, and very illegal. My mind turned straight to Jason Oakland—illegal potions were well within his capabilities—but then pushed the thought aside. I knew what was involved in making this potion. Someone who confused silverweed and white hemstail wouldn't have been able to make a potion that complex, surely.

The potion did make things more interesting, however, in that a witch or a wizard had to make that potion. But who would have hated Blaze that much?

Nothing was coming together on this.

I looked through the rest of the medical file but didn't see anything that might help me solve the murder. Setting it aside, I looked through the desk and found a charging phone. It wouldn't be Chief Enforcer Loeb's; she would have obviously had hers on her. It had to be Blaze's, so I pulled it from the charger and pressed the home button, grinning when I saw it wasn't locked.

I immediately opened up his text messages and found the one in question. It was from Jason.

I have a proposition. Meet at my place, now. I'll make it worth your while.

I raised an eyebrow. What a surprise—Jason had

lied to me. Not only was he not asleep that night the way he had claimed to be, but he was the one who sent Blaze that text. He was the one who had drawn him out in the middle of the night. But that wasn't the most recent text. And it didn't explain the fact that there was an even newer text message on the phone, from around seven in the morning, just a couple of hours before Blaze was murdered.

The second text was sent by an Anne. It had to be Anne Leavis. She was studying to be an assistant Healer, as far as I knew. I couldn't think of anyone else in town named Anne, apart from an old witch in her seventies who was convinced Grandma Rosie was out to get her. Given the context of the message, I figured it wasn't that Anne.

I have to speak to you. Meet me at the usual place? A couple of heart emojis followed immediately after. There was no reply from Blaze, so I wasn't sure if he had actually gone to meet with Anne or not, but I knew exactly who I was speaking with next.

Before I got a chance to put everything back the way it was and get out of there, however, a sound came from outside the door to the office. I froze, not daring to so much as breathe, as I wondered who was coming in. If it was just the shifter, I was fine. After all, the potion was supposed to last for six hours. I still had plenty of time before it wore off.

But as the door to Chief Inspector Loeb's office opened, I found myself looking straight into the eyes of

Jack Stone, who looked, if it was even possible, even more surprised than I was.

"Ali?" he asked, his mouth dropping open.

"Hey, I was looking for the bathroom, and I think I got lost," I said, motioning around the office. Jack recovered himself, crossing his arms and raising an eyebrow at me.

"Looking for the bathroom. Is that right?"

I flashed him the biggest, fakest smile I could. "You know, sometimes you just need to use the little ladies' room."

"At almost eleven o'clock at night. Right."

"To be fair, it's not like I expected the *only* wizard who works in this place to be here this late. What are you doing here, anyway?"

"Really? You want to question me, now? That's where you're going with this? It's a murder investigation. I thought of something, came to check, and heard a sound in the Chief Enforcer's office. Now, if you leave here right now without another word, I won't tell her you were here. But only because I still feel bad about how things ended between us."

I wasn't about to look a gift horse in the mouth. Part of me *really* wanted to know what it was Jack had thought of that brought him here at almost midnight, but even I wasn't dumb enough to open my mouth when he was quite literally giving me a get-out-of-jail-free card.

I slunk past him and out the door, not even turning

back as I slipped out. At least the condition he had attached to my leaving meant I didn't have to thank him for it. I wasn't sure if I would have been able to bring myself to do that.

I practically sprinted home when I left the town hall, my heart pounding in my chest. That was insanely unlucky, for the *only* paranormal who worked at the Enforcers' office who could have seen me to come by just that second.

At least Jack had let me go without reporting me. After all, I had been snooping in his boss's office. He really must have felt bad about how our friendship ended.

I snuck back into the cottage and fell asleep, knowing that in the morning, I had a really good idea as to where to go next in this investigation.

CHAPTER 12

$\mathcal{I}$ woke up the next day full of conviction, eager to get going on the day ahead. After all, I now had a solid lead: Anne Leavis had texted Blaze asking to meet him just a couple of hours before his death. I had seen her at the funeral the day before, and I knew she was studying to be an assistant Healer here in town. I wondered if maybe Willow would make an introduction for me. After all, while I knew of her, I didn't actually know her.

I need to speak to Anne Leavis. Do you know her? I texted Willow as I shoved a slice of toast smothered in jam and butter into my mouth. The reply came a minute later.

Sure. She's quiet, keeps to herself, but I know her. Swing by the hospital around 11 and I'll introduce you; the assistant Healers have their break around then.

I smiled to myself. It was just after nine—I had slept

in a little bit, since I had gotten home so late the night before, but I still had a couple of hours to kill before I had to meet Willow and Anne. I decided to go out for a bit of a walk around the lake, putting on a warm sweater and some leggings and popping on my sunglasses. It was always a good time when it was cold enough to wear a sweater but still bright enough for sunglasses.

I left the cottage, and as I walked down the road, I spotted Grandma Rosie and Connie walking together toward town. A part of me was tempted to follow them, just out of curiosity, but then I realized I was probably happier not knowing what they were up to, and I continued on with my original plan. I began by taking the Lakeside Trail, following the same route from that fateful morning just a few days ago. As soon as I reached the intersection with Space Oddity, however, I noticed a difference. The trail was closed, and an Enforcer stood in front of it, stopping any potential rule breakers from getting past.

"What's going on?" I asked. "Why is the whole trail closed?" After all, I could understand why they closed off the section where Blaze's body had been found, but that was still a significant distance away from here. Why close it this far out?

"It's closed for the safety and integrity of the crime scene," the wolf shifter explained to me. "With the reward offered by the family, we've had altogether too

GOING THROUGH THE POTIONS | 95

many paranormals trying to gain access to the crime scene, so we have closed the entire trail."

My eyebrows raised. "Really? How many people are trying to solve this?"

"By my count, half the town," the shifter said with a sigh. "And a few other paranormals who aren't local, too."

I frowned. Obviously, I should have seen this coming. I wasn't going to be the only paranormal trying to get at that reward money. I suppose a part of me figured it was only crazy people like my grandmother and Connie who were going to take a shot at it, or the completely desperate like myself. But for the Enforcers to shut down an entire trail like that, it was definitely more.

"Plus, security has been stepped up since an intruder made their way into the Enforcers' office last night," the shifter continued.

"Oh?" I asked, raising my eyebrows and doing my best to look as innocent as possible. "Who did it?"

"We're not sure," the shifter replied. "Whoever it was booked it once the Enforcer showed up. They only got a glimpse of the criminal. But now security has been stepped up at all Enforcer locations or anywhere related to this case. I never thought this would be the type of place where we had to be this careful about things."

That was good to know, on two counts. For one thing, it confirmed that Jack kept his word and didn't tell Chief Enforcer Loeb that I had been the one who had broken into the Enforcers' office last night. It was also good to know that trying a second time wasn't a good idea.

I walked away from the shifter, making my way around the lake deep in thought. In a way, maybe this was a good thing. Maybe all I had to do was see what parts of town were now considered off-limits, and I would know where the Enforcers were going with their investigation.

But no, I quickly put that thought out of my head. I needed to investigate this independently, since if I simply followed the Enforcers, they would undoubtedly figure out who committed the crime before me, and that wasn't going to get me any reward money at all.

Still, it was good to know.

CHAPTER 13

At eleven o'clock on the dot I was sitting in the little cafeteria at the hospital. Contrary to standard belief, the food here was actually pretty good, and priced for the fixed income of the majority of their clients. That meant even someone in the ranks of the unemployed—such as myself—could treat themselves to a warm bowl of chili to bring the color back to their cheeks after a crisp cold morning walk.

I was halfway through the bowl when Willow walked toward me, followed by a pretty but shy-looking witch in her early twenties, with copper blonde hair, a small nose, and curious blue eyes. Anne sat in front of me, clasping her hands in her lap and looking down at them immediately.

"Hey, you're Anne, right?" I asked, flashing her a smile that I hoped put her at ease.

Anne nodded in reply.

"Listen, I wanted to say that I'm sorry for your loss," I said to her softly. "I know the relationship between you and Blaze was a secret."

As soon as I said the words, I knew my suspicion had been correct. Anne looked up sharply, fear in her eyes. "Don't worry," I added. "I'm not going to tell anybody. Your secret is safe with me, but I do need to ask you a few questions, since I think it could help me figure out who killed your boyfriend."

Anne didn't answer, so I took that as a sign to keep going.

"How long had you been seeing him?"

"Six months," Anne said in a small voice, barely more than a whisper. "Just over six months."

"And you've been keeping it a secret from everybody," I said softly, treading carefully. After all, I was well aware that a relationship between a dragon and a witch wasn't looked upon very highly by a lot of people in town.

Anne nodded. "That's right. I think my family would have been fine with it. They've always told me that they just want me to be happy. But his family is so old-fashioned. He told me that if they ever found out about it, they would disown him completely. He loved his family. I knew what they meant to him, and I didn't want to do anything to jeopardize the relationship he had with them. So we never told anybody. We always met in secret."

"Did anybody else know about your relationship? Maybe he trusted a close friend?"

This time I got a vehement shake of the head in reply. "Not a chance. I know he didn't even tell his best friend, Daniel. He was too worried that word would somehow get back to his parents. You know what it's like living here. When two people know something, it's not a secret anymore. We were the only ones who knew, and I wouldn't have told anybody, no matter what."

"So how did you meet?" Willow asked, jumping in.

"He hurt himself while volunteering with Keith," Anne explained. "He came into the hospital during one of our classes and offered to let one of the students fix up the cut for him. The professor told me to do it, and I was so nervous that I messed up the spell, and instead of sealing the cut, my spell sealed his mouth shut instead. He couldn't speak, and everyone laughed at me. I was so embarrassed I ran out of the hospital. I was so close to quitting, but Blaze came out and found me, told me that the spell was easily reversed, and told me not to worry about it. He was so nice, and we ended up chatting. The next thing I knew, three hours had passed and the sun had started to go down. He kissed me then, and it felt so right. He told me he wanted to see me again, but that it had to be in secret. We would always meet at the first lookout on Space Oddity."

My eyes widened and I tried not to show it, but I

obviously failed as Anne sighed. "That's where he was killed, isn't it? That's what everyone is saying."

"That's where I found his body," I said softly. "I don't know if he was actually killed there or not."

Anne nodded. "Well, a part of me hopes it was there. That was our happy place, and we had so many good memories there. I'm sure if he had to pick a place to go, that would have been it."

I decided to tackle the sensitive subject of the text she had sent the morning of the murder.

"The morning he was killed, you texted him asking him to meet you at your special place," I began, but Anne's brow furrowed in confusion.

"No, I didn't."

"Are you sure? I saw his phone, and around eight in the morning the day he was killed, there was a text from you asking to meet him."

"That's impossible," Anne replied. "I was here that entire morning; I arrived at six. It was a hands-on day, where we went around and practiced our skills on all the patients in the hospital, so there are something like fifty people who can confirm that I was here that entire time. I never would have gotten a chance to slip away and meet Blaze, so there was no reason for me to send him a text."

She pulled out her phone and handed it to me, showing me the text messages between her and Blaze. The last one had been sent early in the evening the night before his death, a simple heart emoji. The text I had seen in the office on Blaze's phone wasn't there at all. Of course, I knew just how easy it was to delete a text from a phone, but something still didn't add up.

"Anne was here that day," Willow confirmed. "I saw her multiple times as I did my rounds."

Now that really was strange. Something was going on here, and I just wasn't entirely sure what. I couldn't really imagine Anne to be the killer; she seemed to really have loved Blaze. And if Willow confirmed that she was here when Blaze had been murdered, well, I trusted Willow more than anybody on the planet. There was no way Anne could have done it.

Still, Anne would have had the skills to make the poison that killed Blaze. Something wasn't adding up here, and I couldn't quite figure out what it was.

"Can you think of anybody who would have wanted him dead?" I asked, switching tactics. "Did he mention an argument he was having with anybody about anything?"

"He asked me about Jason Oakland," Anne said after a minute's pause. "I had a feeling he wasn't happy about something Jason was doing. I think it might have had something to do with the illegal potions that Jason was selling. A few dragons have ended up in the hospital the last few months after taking them and having adverse effects."

"Oh?" I said, looking at Willow, who nodded in confirmation.

"That's right," Willow said. "Blaze was never one of

them, though. His best friend Daniel was. But that was a couple of months ago. We didn't know who was behind the potions until just now when we found out it was Jason; none of the dragons have ever been willing to tell us, and to be honest, our job is to make them better, not to force them to give up the people who have been supplying them with illegal goods."

"Yeah, Jason confirmed it to me the other day. Blaze found out that Jason's sister had been taking the stuff and told him to stop."

Willow raised her eyebrows. "Wow, that's definitely news. I knew he was a scumbag, but I didn't know he was the one responsible for making all of those bad potions. When Anne told us, I was very surprised."

"Did Bridget ever end up in the hospital?" I asked.

Willow shook her head. "Not as far as I know. She must have never gotten a bad batch."

I frowned. I still thought Jason was the most likely culprit for this murder. But things just didn't add up. Where did the text from Anne that wasn't on her phone fit in? If Jason had wanted to kill Blaze, I figured he would have just texted him himself. After all, Jason wasn't smart enough to cover his tracks like that, I didn't think. Besides, Jason had texted Blaze the night before asking to meet him. Why wouldn't he have just killed Blaze then?

There were just so many questions left that I had no answer to.

I thanked Anne for speaking with me, and she

nodded. She got up to go but stopped as soon as she stood up.

"Please find the person who did this," she told me. "I know Blaze's family put up a lot of money to find the killer, and I know that's probably why you're doing this, but out of everybody who's been hanging around trying to get information from the Healers to see what they can find out, you're the only person who has found me. I want you to get to the bottom of this, for his sake. He was a good dragon, and I miss him already. I don't have any money to offer, but I hope that you get the reward if you find the killer."

"I'll do my best," I said earnestly. "And your secret is safe with me. No one is going to find out about your relationship from these lips."

Anne nodded. "I appreciate that. We always knew that if we were going to get more serious, we were eventually going to have to tell everybody. But it never got to that point. I think it would have. I'm not sure how to handle that, but now that he's gone, I would be happier if no one found out."

"I understand completely," I replied. Anne gave me a small smile and headed back into the depths of the hospital to continue her classes.

"I still can't believe it was Jason making those potions the whole time," Willow mused, eyeing the other half of my bowl of chili.

I pushed it over to her, and she immediately

grinned, grabbing the spoon and taking a huge mouthful.

"Yeah, it was him. Which probably explains why so many dragons ended up in the hospital if that's who he was mainly selling to. He sucks as a wizard, and so probably messed up the potions a few times, which would have led to adverse effects."

"What an idiot," Willow said with her mouth full. She swallowed, then continued. "I've seen a few of the cases of dragons who took bad potions. They halluci- nate like crazy and start basically going insane. We have to get the antidote into them as soon as possible. The problem is, sometimes, in their delirium, they end up shifting. Luckily, the only time we had a dragon send a giant fireball down a hallway was at three in the morning, so nobody was hurt. Chief Enforcer Loeb has been looking into who's been doing it, but of course, if no one is willing to give up the seller, there is not a lot she can do. I can always tip her off, now that I know."

"I wonder why nobody was giving up Jason," I mused. "And I wonder how Blaze found out it was him."

"I bet Blaze went and bought some of the potion just to find out who is selling it," Willow said. "After all, that sounds exactly like him, especially since his best friend and his sister had both used it, and his best friend ended up here once."

I nodded. Willow was right; buying the potion to find out who the seller was did sound exactly like

Blaze. Still, why not go straight to Chief Enforcer Loeb? I wished I knew a dragon well enough to ask about the process, then realized maybe Bridget would be willing to help me.

After all, she had bought from Jason. She would be able to tell me exactly how his system worked, and maybe fill in some of the answers.

"I need to speak with his sister," I said to Willow.

"And I need to get back to the wizard who accidentally managed to make his eyes disappear," Willow replied. "The potion to make them grow back should be finished in a couple of minutes, so I'm sure he'll be relieved to have his sight back."

"If he waits a couple of months though, he'd have the most epic Halloween costume ever," I said with a grin, and Willow laughed.

"That's for sure. The other day, a lion shifter cub accidentally ran into his room, took one look at the wizard's empty eye sockets, and ran out the other way screaming. His mother told him that's what happens when you go exploring by yourself."

This time it was my turn to laugh. Willow bussed the tray with the chili, thanked me for letting her eat it —"I've been working for the last twelve hours without a break, so I was ravenous"—and the two of us split up once more with the promise to get dinner soon so I could catch her up on everything.

I was going to go find Bridget and see if I couldn't get a few more answers.

CHAPTER 14

I made my way back to the caves, only to be told by the shifter guarding the entrance that Bridget had gone out for a fly to try and clear her head. I made my way back home, questions turning over in my head.

To my chagrin, as soon as I reached the cottage, I saw a face I definitely didn't want to see. It was Jack, standing on my mother's front stoop, along with another wizard. Had Jack broken up with Sean already? If he had, I was going to stab him. The least he could do after completely breaking my heart and then grinding it into a fine dust for good measure was to have a long-lasting relationship with my ex.

Curiosity overtook hatred as the dominant emotion and I made my way toward the front door.

"What's going on here?" I asked, with Jack and the other wizard turning toward me. They were chatting with my mom, who looked even more haggard than usual.

"We were just saying goodbye to your mother," Jack said. "Thank you again for your assistance."

"I swear, I don't know what's wrong with her," my mom said, shaking her head. "I'm sorry. I'll try and knock some sense into her."

She closed the door, and I found myself facing the other two wizards. Not that I really noticed Jack. I was fixated on the other one, who I didn't recognize. He was tall, a few inches over six feet, with sandy blond hair that was messed up just enough to give him a permanent bedhead look. His blue eyes glimmered with curiosity as they looked at me. He was dressed similarly to Jack, with form-fitting clothes that revealed just enough of his body to confirm that he spent a lot of time at the gym.

I swore, some men got all the luck.

"And who is this?" I asked, motioning to the new guy.

"This is Andrew," Jack said with a small smile.

"Please, call me Andy," the wizard replied, holding out a hand. His Australian drawl was long and, I had to admit, super sexy. I took his hand, looking up at him curiously.

"So what were the two of you doing here?" I asked. "And what does Grandma Rosie have to do with anything?"

"Unfortunately, your grandmother and Connie

were caught attempting to steal files from Enforcer headquarters," Jack said, tilting his head slightly. "Apparently, word that security was beefed up after an intrusion the night before didn't quite make it to them."

"Oh, really," I said, raising my eyebrows slightly.

"I was surprised, really. I thought someone as, erm, well-connected as your grandmother would have heard about what had happened."

I understood what was happening here. Andy didn't know that I was the intruder in question, and Jack didn't want him to know about it.

"I suppose my grandmother isn't as well-connected as you thought, then," I replied. "She's a little bit of a lone wolf. Well, a wolf duo, if you count Connie. But our family prefers to work alone on things."

Jack nodded in understanding. "I guess that must be it. Luckily, she and Connie were contrite enough that Chief Enforcer Loeb decided not to press charges."

"I guess that runs in the family too," I said with a grin, earning myself a warning glance from Jack. I supposed he wasn't close enough to this new boy toy of his to have told him about what had happened. How long had they been together? It couldn't have been long; I had only caught Sean and Jack a few months back. Maybe things between them weren't serious.

Wait, what did I care? I was pissed off at Jack for how he'd treated me.

"Alright, well, that's everything here. Thanks," Jack said officially with a formal nod.

"It was nice to meet you," Andy said to me with a smile.

"It was *very* nice to meet you, too," I replied. Why did all the super-hot wizards have to be gay? Things just weren't fair sometimes.

I frowned to myself as Jack and Andy made their way down the street. They kept a professional distance from one another; I hadn't heard of Jack and Sean breaking up, so I imagined that when they were out in public, they made an effort not to show their affection.

Where was Andy from, anyway? He wasn't local to Mt. Rheanier. I knew that much. It wasn't just the fact that I knew every member of our coven, or the fact that everything about Andy screamed water coven. It helped that he had a foreign accent. No one who grows up in Washington ends up sounding Australian. Not even by accident.

I was going to have to ask around, see what people knew about this new blossoming relationship. There was a time when Jack would have called and told me everything, and a tiny, tiny little part of me pined for those days. But then the reasonable part of me took over and declared that Jack was as good as dead to me, and that if I ever found myself in close proximity to a knife while he was around, he'd be dead to everyone else, too.

I paused outside my cottage but didn't go inside. After all, no one ever made half a million abras by sitting around watching TV because the person they wanted to speak to wasn't around. I was just going to have to find Bridget myself.

I instead grabbed a broom from the side of the cottage and soared into the sky. This wasn't a thing I did often. I was an earth coven witch. I was happier with my feet planted firmly on the ground, but I also wasn't *bad* on the broom. I gripped the handle a little bit harder than an air coven witch might have, sure, but I also didn't get dizzy when I looked down.

I let the air whip my hair around as I wondered if maybe I shouldn't have grabbed a thicker sweater before zipping through the sky. I decided against turning back and grabbing one; this was a perfect excuse to make a nice hot chocolate when I got home.

I soared up about two hundred feet and started looking around as I flew above the lake. My eyes scanned the skies, looking for the shape of a dragon that might be Bridget. It was funny; I had actually never really looked at the landscape from this vantage point. I could see everything from here. A couple of witches having a picnic along the beach despite the cold weather, the shimmer of the sun on the lake, the top of Mt. Rheanier, even the lookout where I had seen Blaze's body. There was a shifter standing at the lookout now, obviously making sure no paranormals got too close to where the body had been found in an attempt to get clues.

I knew the dragons liked being close to the mountain, so I turned my broom to face Mt. Rheanier. I made my way around the mountain, circling it a few times but seeing no sign of Bridget. On my third pass around, just as I was telling myself I should just give up and go home, I spotted a glimmer through the trees as the sun's rays caught on a couple of black and yellow scales.

I couldn't guarantee it was Bridget—I was pretty bad at telling the shifters apart when they were in their animal forms—but figured it was a pretty good shot and flew down to the clearing where she was curled up.

"Bridget?" I asked from a safe distance when I landed, my hand on my broom, ready to fly back up into the sky on a moment's notice. After all, the dragon looked like it was sleeping, and I wasn't entirely sure how waking up a sleeping dragon was going to go for me. It wasn't the sort of thing I did on a regular basis.

The dragon's eye opened, and a moment later Bridget shifted back into her human form. Relief washed over me as I realized it was actually her. "Hi," Bridget said to me. "What are you doing here?"

"Looking for you," I replied. "I was wondering if I could ask you a few things."

"I guess. I came out here looking for a bit of peace. Everyone always looks at me with sadness in their eyes. They all walk on eggshells around me. No one mentions Blaze at all, except to tell me how sorry they are. I just hate it all so much. I feel like an ingrate reacting like this, since I know everyone means well, but at the same time, I don't really know how I feel, you know? I'm just so angry someone did this to him, and I want them caught."

I nodded. I had been young when my father died, young enough that I never really knew him or understood what was going on. I had a few memories of the funeral, but they were mostly blurred impressions more than distinct memories. I hadn't lost anybody close to me since I was old enough to really understand death, but I could imagine how confusing it must have felt to Bridget.

"I heard that you were a frequent user of Jason Oakland's potions," I started, and Bridget narrowed her eyes at me.

"Who told you that?"

I shrugged. "Word gets around. Listen, I don't care. As far as I'm concerned, do what you want with your own life. But is it true?"

Bridget eyed me for a minute, as if trying to decide whether to tell me the truth, then eventually came to a conclusion. She sighed, her shoulders dropping as she looked at the ground. "Yeah. I wouldn't say I'm a frequent user, though. I just do it sometimes. It's rough living in a small town, you know? Especially when you don't need to work. I just kind of feel empty a lot of the time, and the potions make me really feel alive, you know?"

"Did you know that other dragons ended up in the hospital after taking them? Jason isn't exactly the world's most talented wizard."

"Yeah, I know. I'm friends with a witch—she works as an assistant Healer—she always tests mine for me. She knows I take them, since she takes them with me. That way, because she can test them before we take them, we never get sick."

Another assistant Healer? My eyebrows rose. I wondered what the odds were that Bridget and Anne Leavis were friends. "What's the name of your friend?" I asked.

"Kirsten Dail."

I frowned. So it wasn't Anne. The fact that they were both assistant Healers must have been a coincidence.

"Did you know that Blaze had been arguing with Jason about the potions? He didn't want Jason selling to you anymore."

Bridget gave me a sad smile. "I did know, yes. I'm sure Blaze wanted to keep it a secret, but Jason came to me a few days ago. He told me he wasn't going to be able to sell to me anymore. Wouldn't tell me why, but I knew. It was exactly the sort of thing Blaze would have done."

"Weren't you mad at your brother?"

Bridget shook her head. "No, not really. I mean, sure, it was going to be more difficult for me to get potions. And the night before he died, I told him to stay out of my business." She stared off into space for a minute, her eyes watering. I imagined that conversation may have been the last one she'd ever had with her brother. "But the reality was, I didn't depend on the potions. I wasn't addicted, the way some other paranormals are. I took them on occasion, and this just meant that I was going to have to find a different supplier in a different town. It wasn't going to make my life all that much more difficult. Besides, you're right about Jason. He's a terrible wizard, and frankly, the quality of his potions had gone downhill the last few months anyway. Three times Kirsten found batches that would have landed us in the hospital if we'd taken them. It was time to move on from Jason as a supplier no matter what."

I looked at Bridget carefully as she said the words, but she definitely appeared to be telling the truth.

"Do you know why Jason's quality had gone down?"

Bridget shrugged. "Don't have a clue."

"Ok," I said, deciding to change tactics. "Did you know Blaze was in a relationship?"

Bridget's eyebrows rose. "No, he definitely wasn't."

"He was; I spoke to her myself and I saw messages between them."

"Her?" Bridget said. "No way."

This time it was my turn to give Bridget a small smile. "You thought your brother was gay."

"I did," Bridget confirmed. "I always thought he had a thing for Daniel. Daniel is the most promiscuous dragon in town, though, and only goes for the ladies. You're saying Blaze had a thing for a female dragon?"

"She wasn't a dragon, but yes."

Bridget shook her head. "No, he wouldn't have dated outside of the species. Not a chance."

"Well, he did. He kept it secret since he was afraid of what your parents would think."

"They would have hated it for sure," Bridget said. "I mean, I don't really care either way, but our parents are old-fashioned. That's why I always thought he was staying in the closet, too."

To be totally honest, I didn't see what it was about Blaze that made Bridget think he was gay. But then again, given my own romantic history, someone had obviously gone to town on my gaydar with a baseball bat at some point. What did I know?

"So you had no idea he was dating a witch."

"None at all," Bridget said, shaking her head.

"Ok," I said. "Thanks. If you think of anything else, come and find me, ok?"

"Yeah," Bridget replied.

I went to fly back toward town, but then stopped. "Do you know how close anyone else is to solving this?" I asked.

Bridget shrugged. "I've spoken to a few people. Your grandmother and Connie were here the other day, asking me about Daniel. But to be completely honest, I have no idea."

"Ok, thanks. Oh, and just one more thing," I continued, a thought popping into my brain.

"Yeah?"

"Did Blaze know that the quality of the potions you were taking had gone down recently?"

"I don't see how. I certainly didn't tell him."

I nodded, getting ready to fly back to town.

"Wait," Bridget said suddenly, and I looked at her expectantly.

"Can you keep what you know about Blaze and his relationship private? It's not about me," she added quickly. "I just don't want our parents to find out. It would break their heart, and I'd just rather they never find out about it, you know?"

"Yeah," I replied with a nod. "No problem. It'll just be between us." I could understand Bridget not wanting her parents to have to go through any more pain and suffering than they were already feeling. I flew back off toward town, deep in thought. Bridget hadn't told Blaze that Jason's potions were getting worse, but I could think of one more person who might have done so.

$\mathcal{I}$ immediately made my way back to the hospital and found Willow.

"Do you know how hard it is to try and communicate with a wizard who turned his head into a giant dandelion?" Willow asked me. "I had to try and figure out exactly how he did it so I could reverse the spell, and let me tell you, it was not easy."

I smiled at the thought. "Well, I imagine it ended well?"

"Yeah, dandelion-head is back to being old Cameron Kilmer."

"Let me guess, he was trying to make his plants grow bigger, and it all went awry?"

"You got it," Willow grinned. Cameron was an amateur gardener—emphasis on the amateur—who was convinced he was Rhea's gift to gardening and had recently begun attempting to enter the local largest gourd competition, in which the best gardeners in the Pacific Northwest got together and showed off their biggest pumpkins, squashes, and zucchinis. The competition was taking place in a couple of weeks, and it looked like Cameron was trying to give his plants a nudge in the wrong direction.

"On the bright side, if dandelions were a gourd, I probably could have left him that way for a couple of weeks and he would have romped it in," Willow said. "It was literally the size of his face. And his neck had turned into a green stalk, too."

"That's so weird," I said with a shudder. "I'm glad I don't do what you do."

"Well, I'm pretty sure magical fixers have to deal with gross magic too," Willow said. "So you'd better get used to my war stories."

"Right. That's if I even need the money after I blow this case wide open. Is Anne around? I have a quick question I need to ask her."

"Sure, the students will be leaving for the day soon. Wait by the exit and she'll come out that way."

I thanked Willow and made my way to a bench at the hospital entrance. Sure enough, about ten minutes later, a handful of witches and wizards with the requisite "A" stamped onto their uniforms, along with a smaller "S" designating them to be students, made their way through the doors, looking harried and ready for a good night's sleep.

Anne was one of the last of them to come through,

walking slowly, looking down at the ground. She looked ready to burst into tears at any moment. My heart broke for her; it couldn't have been easy having to grieve in secret the way she was doing.

"Hey, Anne," I said to her softly as she walked past me. Maybe too softly; the witch jumped about a foot in the air as she spotted me.

"Oh. Ali, hi," she said.

"Listen, I was wondering if I could ask you a quick question."

"Sure, of course."

"Did you tell Blaze that the potions Jason had been making were getting worse and worse? That more dragons were ending up in the hospital after taking them?"

"I sure did," Anne nodded. "Well, I told him it seemed that way, anyway. It was possible there were just more of them out there, which would have meant the same percentage of bad batches would have still landed more dragons in the hospital overall. But we did have a discussion about it, around a week ago. He was worried about his sister."

"Do you know a witch studying with you, Kirsten Dail?"

"Yeah, I know Kirsten," Anne confirmed.

"Was she here the morning Blaze was killed?" I asked. I didn't really suspect Kirsten—I really had abso-lutely no reason to—but while I was here, I figured I might as well rule whoever I possibly could out as a suspect.

"She was, I saw her that morning," Anne said with a nod. "Why, do you think she might have had anything to do with this?"

"No, not really," I admitted. "I just found out she was friends with Bridget, Blaze's sister, and so I'm checking out everyone just in case."

"Oh, sure," Anne said. "But no, she was here that morning. In fact, she messed up a simple spell used to clean wounds and managed to accidentally make a vampire's cut shoot out ninja stars. It was crazy; we had to try and get access to his wound so that we could staunch the stars without getting hit by them. No one told me when I went to become an assistant Healer that I'd also have to be a martial arts expert."

Anne even ventured a little bit of a laugh before quickly clamping her mouth shut, as though realizing she was still grieving and not supposed to be having any fun.

"Well, that sounds awful," I said.

"It was. I mean, in hindsight we laughed about it. Kirsten felt so bad about what had happened. We're all just under a lot of pressure; we have a set of exams coming up and she told me she'd been up the whole night studying. She just wasn't thinking when she cast the spell."

"Yeah, we've all been there," I said with a grin. Exam stress was no joke. When I was back at the Academy, I had once been so stressed that when I tried to make a potion that would calm a crying baby, it made anyone who drank it burst into tears. Needless to say, I didn't get a passing mark on that particular assignment.

"Does this mean you're no closer to finding the killer?" Anne asked sadly.

"I have a pretty good idea as to who did it," I said. "It's just a matter of proving it."

The more I discovered, the more I thought Jason had to be the one behind it. After all, he had reason to want Blaze dead, he had no alibi, and who knew— maybe he did manage to properly make the potion that killed Blaze. Even a broken clock was right twice a day.

Now I just had to find proof—and do it before Chief Enforcer Loeb and her crew got there first.

"Good," Anne said to me. "I hope whoever did it rots in jail forever."

"Me too," I replied. "Thanks again for the help."

Anne nodded and stalked off, and I sat back down on the bench, watching her form fade off into the distance. A couple of minutes later, Willow joined me.

"So how'd it go?"

"Yeah, good. I'm sure Jason is the killer. He just has to be."

"You just have to prove it?"

I nodded. "That's an issue. I have no idea how I'm going to do that. I guess the best way would be to find the potion he used to kill Blaze. There can't have been any evidence on the knife, or the Enforcers would have already arrested him, and if anyone saw him go after Blaze in the forest, then they would have come forward already."

"In that case, yeah, I think finding the potion Jason used is your best bet."

I nodded, staring distractedly at the ground. Something still didn't add up. I didn't like the fact that Anne said she didn't text Blaze that morning. Had Jason managed to spoof her phone somehow, to set a trap for Blaze? Had Anne been lying to me, and she had sent the message?

That was the only question mark I still had. Everything else pointed to Jason. It had to be him, then. I was just missing something, I was sure of it. But hey, as long as I had the right guy, all I had to do was find proof he was the killer, and I'd be happy.

"So what's your plan to find the potion?"

"I don't know," I said slowly. "A part of me thinks I should break into his house and see if I can find proof he made the poison that killed Blaze."

"Well, at least your plan is totally legal."

"Hey, if you want to make a half-million-abra omelet, you're going to have to break a few eggs. Besides, it's not like I can get caught breaking and entering twice in one week. That would just be bad luck."

Willow raised an eyebrow. "There was a first time?"

I had completely forgotten to tell her about the other night, and by the time I had finished recounting the story, Willow was laughing so hard tears streamed down her face as she clutched her side.

"You're literally the only person that would ever happen to," she said. "Did you seriously tell him you were just looking for the bathroom?"

I shrugged. "I didn't know what else to do."

"You're insane. I can't believe Jack let you go."

"Yeah. Me neither. He must really feel bad about me seeing his bare butt."

"That must be it," Willow giggled. "Or he misses being friends with you."

"Well, maybe he should have thought about that before stealing my boyfriend."

"Anyway, I'm glad you weren't arrested. You'd probably still be in jail right now if you'd actually been caught. I can't believe you did that!"

"Yeah, well, I need that money."

"Speaking of, I asked around. They're currently looking to hire a witch or a wizard in janitorial here," Willow said. "It doesn't pay well, and it's not the best work, but it is a job."

I nodded. "Thanks." Honestly, I'd rather stab myself in the face than spend the day cleaning up weird paranormal hospital goo, but I did appreciate that Willow looked into it for me. The fact that I might have to actually consider applying for the job anyway only fueled my desire to find proof Jason was behind this murder and claim that reward money.

After all, half a million abras would easily get me

through the next six months until I could try the magical fixer test again, and then leave some left over so I could start saving up for that place I wanted to buy my mom.

"Well, if you're going to do it, I'm coming with you."

I raised an eyebrow. "Really? Breaking and entering doesn't really seem to be your sort of thing."

"It shouldn't be anyone's *thing*," Willow said, giving me a hard look. "But since you insist on getting yourself arrested in the course of trying to find out who did this, the least I can do is try and help."

"Thanks," I said with a grin.

"But if we find the proof and you get that money, you're buying the celebratory dinner."

"Deal."

CHAPTER 16

I did my best to avoid being seen by my mother for the rest of the day. I didn't want an invitation to dinner, as I figured it was going to be at least a couple of days before Mom and Grandma Rosie stopped fighting over my grandmother's arrest. I sent Leda a text, warning her to avoid home for a couple of days.

Why, what happened? my sister replied a moment later.

Grandma Rosie got caught breaking into the Enforcers' office and Mom isn't happy about it.

Leda responded with three horrified-looking emojis. A second later, another reply appeared. *Are you serious?*

One hundred percent. Steer clear for a while.

Thanks for the warning.

Willow and I had planned to meet just after dark at

a park not far from Jason's place. I tried to dress in dark clothes that would hide me from sight as much as possible, while at the same time doing my best not to look like I was getting ready for a night of lawbreaking. I figured I managed to straddle that line pretty well as I made my way out into the night, tucking my wand into my pocket for good measure. I could have used an invisibility spell, sure, but if anyone around was using spell detection methods, I'd be caught, *and* I'd look a lot more suspicious than if I pretended I was just going for a late-night walk on my own.

I slipped past the cottage, looking through the lit windows to see Grandma Rosie looking defiant and my mother looking defeated, and smiled to myself. I was definitely glad I hadn't been involved in that particular discussion, and even *more* glad that my mom had no idea I'd been caught doing exactly the same thing as Grandma Rosie just a few hours earlier.

As I reached the park, I spotted Willow shadow-boxing in the sandbox, the focus on her face intense.

"Practicing for tonight?"

"You can never be too careful," Willow said to me. I couldn't help but notice even in the dim light of the full moon that her face was pale. This was definitely outside of her comfort zone.

"You don't have to do this with me," I said, but Willow shook her head.

"If it's going to help you, I want to do it. It's stupid that you lost your job, and you didn't deserve that.

GOING THROUGH THE POTIONS | 127

Besides, I'm a good influence on you. Hopefully with me around you won't do anything too stupid."

"Alright. Well, I can't really deny that, can I? Anyway, I was thinking we cast a spell to put Jason to sleep, go in, and have a look around."

"And that right there is why I'm here," Willow said, crossing her arms. "We're not going to cast a spell on anyone. If you do, he's going to wake up, realize someone put a spell on him, and if he's guilty, he might run. Or he might go to the Enforcers, and you're going to be the first person Jack is going to think of."

"Second, actually," I replied. "Grandma Rosie and Connie will be first."

Willow shot me a look. "Fine," I said, throwing my hands in the air. "We do it your way. What's your plan? Sit in this park and wait until he dies of old age?"

"No, but I do think we should get a good vantage point and try to spy on him. If we climb that tree, we should get a pretty good look through his window. Who knows what we'll see?"

"Paint drying, probably," I muttered. Maybe this was one of those hammer-versus-scalpel things, though. I couldn't help but think that maybe doing things Willow's way would be a good way to learn the finesse and patience that I would need as a magical fixer. What was the worst that could happen? An early death caused by boredom, I supposed.

"Fine," I muttered, making my way to the tree in question. It was a large pine tree; the thick foliage would keep us hidden, but we'd still be able to see straight through Jason's living room window if we climbed up a couple of feet. I jumped up and grabbed the lowest branch, my feet dangling as I tried and failed to hoist myself upward. Eventually, I reached my feet over to the tree's trunk and climbed them upward until I was hanging off the branch like a sloth. With a bunch of awkward maneuvers, I eventually managed to roll my body onto the branch and sit up.

"Some witches can't do that elegantly," Willow teased, and I flipped her off as she swung effortlessly up onto the branch. I would never admit it to her, but I was totally jealous of how gracefully she had managed that.

Willow moved next to me, and the two of us peered through the branches and into Jason's home. The lights were on and the blinds open, which made it super simple to see what was going on inside. Jason was on the phone, gesticulating to someone while he paced around the room.

"Talking to his lawyer, who's trying to convince him to turn himself in?" I suggested.

"That wouldn't be good news for you," Willow pointed out.

"Alright, then he's trying to hire a prostitute, but she wants to charge him double for being so gross."

Willow snickered. "Now that's much more realistic."

Eventually Jason hung up the phone and tossed it onto the table. Plonking himself down on the couch, he grabbed the remote for the TV, hoisted his legs up onto the coffee table, and settled himself in.

"Well, looks like we're going to be here a while," I said with a sigh. "Time to settle in."

"Look on the bright side. It could be raining," Willow pointed out.

I laughed. "That's very true." We lived in the Pacific Northwest, after all. When the sun was out and the weather crisp in the fall, I absolutely loved it. When there was a torrential downpour that lasted for days, I loved it just a little bit less. Unfortunately, the latter was far too common.

But hey, tonight the weather really was nice. The full moon even meant everything outside wasn't completely shrouded in darkness.

I figured I might as well find out what I could from Willow while we had some time.

"Do you know an assistant Healer student named Kirsten? Kirsten Dail?"

Willow frowned next to me. "Oh, maybe? I think I've run into her once or twice. I've seen her around at the hospital, but I can't say I really know her. Why?"

"Oh, no real reason. She's friends with Bridget, Blaze's sister, that's all."

"Do you think she has something to do with this?"

I shrugged. "Honestly, I have no reason to think that. She was at the hospital that morning, when Blaze was killed, so she couldn't have done it."

"But something is bothering you anyway."

"I don't like the fact that no one seems to know where the text message from Anne's phone to Blaze came from."

"Well, I've always been a strong believer in the idea that if it looks like a duck and quacks like a duck, it's a duck."

"So you think Anne sent it."

"Probably," Willow said. "What are the other options?"

"Someone could have spoofed her number somehow and sent the message from elsewhere," I suggested. "That's possible, right?"

"I mean, sure, I guess theoretically it's possible, but it would have to be someone who knows a lot about technology. And I don't know that much about Jason, but I'm going to go out on a limb and assume "good with technology" doesn't exactly describe him."

"Yeah," I frowned. "Otherwise, someone could have physically taken Anne's phone, sent the message, deleted it from her phone, and then put the phone back in her pocket."

"That's actually more realistic, I think," Willow replied. "But it still comes with some issues. How would they have managed it without Anne noticing? How would they have managed it without anyone else noticing?"

"That's all I've got. The only other option is that Anne sent the message herself. But why? Why would she do that? She couldn't leave the hospital, so she had no reason to get Blaze to meet her."

"Unless it wasn't her Blaze was supposed to meet," Willow said, her eyes meeting mine. I shuddered at the thought.

"Do you really think Anne could be the killer? But she seems so...I don't know, quiet. She doesn't seem the type to poison her boyfriend, then stab him in the back."

"It's the quiet ones you have to watch out for," Willow said to me, wiggling her eyebrows up and down at me.

"Oh, yeah, I'm sure you're going to be breaking into my house in the middle of the night and stabbing me one day," I replied. "That definitely sounds like you."

"Ok, fine. It's not me. But my point is, you don't know who the killer is. It could be anyone. It could be Anne. Maybe she left the potion there for him to eat, maybe inside some chocolates or something, and then had someone else stab him."

"Now who's coming up with crazy ideas?" I grinned.

"Hey, we're sitting in a tree in the middle of the night spying on a guy who's obviously in the middle of the world's most boring Netflix marathon. I'm not sure either one of us gets to play the sanity card right now."

"Fair enough," I laughed.

"So think about Anne. What reason could she have had for wanting Blaze dead?"

"Well, that's the thing, she doesn't have one. They were in a relationship, she seemed to very much like him, and now she's super sad because he's dead."

Willow shook her head. "You need to watch more bad television. We only know they were together because *that's what she told us*. What if Blaze broke up with her? No one else knew about their relationship, so all she would have had to do was lie to us, and there was no one else who could confirm or deny her story. If they broke up and she decided to get her revenge in the deadliest way possible, who would know?"

I gasped so hard I nearly fell out of the tree, gripping the branch to steady myself. "Seriously? Anne? That little quiet thing? I mean, I guess you're right, but I just can't imagine it."

Before I had a chance to mull over Willow's words further, though, Jason suddenly checked his phone, turned off the TV, and got up. The two of us were rapt with attention as he went to the kitchen, moving out of our line of sight for a minute, then returned a minute later with a small cooler bag. Grabbing his shoes, he moved toward the front door.

"Looks like he's going out," Willow said, and I nodded.

"Yeah. I wonder where. It's almost midnight."

"Should we follow him?"

I shook my head. "No, I don't think so. I want to see what's inside his place. If we can find proof that he had the poison in there, then we've got him."

"Ok, good plan," Willow said. Jason made his way to the front door, turned off the lights, locked up, and walked down the street. The fact that he walked and didn't take a broom meant he wasn't necessarily going super far, unless he was going to take the portal elsewhere. I had no idea how long we were going to have until he came back. We were going to have to be quick.

CHAPTER 17

"Time for an invisibility spell," I said to Willow.

"I brought potions just in case," she replied, pulling out a couple small vials from a pocket. Perfect. I took one from her and swallowed it, immediately disappearing.

"How long will this last?" I asked.

"Two hours," Willow said. "I figured we might need them."

"Good thinking."

We made our way to Jason's building. I headed to the front door, pulling out my wand, just in case. Unfortunately, it appeared multitasking wasn't my strong suit, and taking out my wand and going up the stairs leading to the door didn't go well together. I tripped on the top step and fell straight into Willow, who let out a small yelp, the two of us falling against the building's front door with a thud.

"Rhea above, you scared the crap out of me!" Willow hissed.

"Sorry," I said sheepishly.

"We're trying not to get caught here," Willow pointed out.

"I'll let my two left feet know," I replied.

Willow carefully opened the front door to the building and slipped inside. I closed the door behind me and we stood still for a moment, taking in the surroundings. The lobby was low-ceilinged and dark, with a couple of upholstered chairs in the corner that looked like they hadn't been replaced since the eighties. The lightbulb above flashed intermittently; maintenance didn't exactly seem to be a priority in this building.

"Let's get going. I feel like I'm in a horror movie here," Willow whispered to me, and I nodded. The two of us headed down the hallway to the left, stopping in front of the first door on the left, which had to be Jason's, given the location of his windows.

"Ready?" I asked.

"To commit my first-ever felony?" Willow said. "My mom was right—you are a bad influence."

"I'll take that as a yes," I said as I cast a quick spell to get rid of any wards, then opened the door and stepped into the apartment. I turned on the entry light and had a look around.

The money Jason Oakland saved on rent by living in this dump should have been invested into a cleaning service. I scrunched up my nose as I looked around. Why was there an old slice of pizza crust on the ground next to his shoes in the entryway? Did he even *own* a broom? I had so many questions.

"We're going to die from botulism just by spending time in here," Willow muttered. "Hold on, I'm going to go close the curtains so we can turn the lights on in the rest of this place."

About thirty seconds later, the rest of the lights in the apartment flickered on, and I stepped through the entryway into the kitchen. It was just as dirty in there; dishes were piled high in the sink, the counter had a glob of jam so old it was developing white spots, and the smell made me want to run away and never come back.

"It's a miracle he hasn't killed himself by accident," I muttered as I looked at the fridge. I was legitimately scared as to what I was going to find in there. I wasn't expecting to find a severed head or anything like that; I was much more terrified of a year-old milk carton or something.

I held my breath as I opened the fridge door. I figured this would be the ideal spot to store poisonous potions. Some potions had to be stored at room temperature, but much like regular food, most potions kept longer if they were in the fridge.

Of course, that was assuming that Jason kept some

of the potion. If he was smart, he would have dumped it down the sink as soon as he'd killed Blaze. But then, this was Jason Oakland we were talking about. He wasn't exactly a candidate for the paranormal branch of Mensa.

The fridge was in exactly the shape I was expecting. Old food was so solidly plastered on the plastic shelves that they had basically molded into the plastic, and frankly, I was tempted to just burn down this whole apartment in the name of public safety.

My eyes were immediately drawn to four different cauldrons, however. They were all filled with different-colored potions.

"Willow," I called out, and I heard a reply a minute later.

"Don't go into the bathroom. I've seen things I can't unsee."

I laughed. "Did you by any chance bring any extra vials?"

"To collect samples of any potions we found so we could test them for poison later? Because you didn't think to do it? Why yes, yes I did."

"I knew I was your friend for a reason," I grinned. "Hand them over."

It took a second or two of maneuvering—because Willow had had the vials on her when we took the potion, they were invisible as well—but eventually Willow handed me four glass vials, which I filled with a bit of each potion and stoppered before slipping them into my pocket.

"What do you think?" I asked. "Poison?"

"Could be," Willow said. "I don't recognize any of those by sight, and I'm pretty good at telling my potions apart these days."

"Ok, we'll see when we get home," I replied. "Did you have a look around the rest of this place?"

"I did," Willow nodded. "Couldn't find anything else. Should we get out of here?"

"Yeah," I said, but a second later, the front door to the apartment creaked open. I stared wide-eyed at where I knew Willow was standing, even though I couldn't see her. Jason was back.

"What do we do?" Willow whispered.

"I don't know," I replied. "Try and get out of here without him touching us."

I slipped toward the hallway and looked down at the open door, and as soon as I did, my blood turned to ice.

Jason wasn't there. In fact, there was no one there. That meant there was another intruder in here. Someone else who had turned themselves invisible was now in this apartment with us.

I moved back and grabbed Willow by what I thought was her wrist and pulled her deeper into the kitchen.

"There's someone else in here," I whispered as quietly as I could.

"What do we do?" she replied.

I shrugged before realizing a second later there was no way Willow could see my reaction.

"What if it's linked to the murder?" I asked. "We need to find out who it is."

"Ok, we have to break their spell. Let's split up. We can't let them know we're here."

"Yup."

With that, Willow and I broke apart. I moved carefully through the apartment. After all, if I hit the person who was in here with us, that would let them know they weren't alone in here. I managed to squeeze myself into a small gap between the fridge and the wall while I waited for the intruder to come into the kitchen; there was no way they would bother to check the gap I was in for any reason.

My plan was to wait for the intruder to come into the kitchen and make a sound, or maybe open the fridge door or a cupboard. When they did that, I would jump out, cast a paralyzing spell, and then reverse their invisibility spell so that I could see who it was.

It was perfect. Well, apart from one tiny flaw. Sure enough, the intruder came into the kitchen. I could just make out their footsteps as they walked past me, and I held my breath, not daring to so much as breathe lest my presence be discovered. I jumped out from my hiding spot, pulling out my wand and preparing to cast my spell, but my foot got caught under the fridge and instead I fell to the floor with a bang, hitting my arm and dropping my wand.

Ugh. This was *so* not my best moment.

"Get out of here!" I called out, hoping Willow would get the hint, but hoping the intruder would also think I was speaking to them. I pulled on my leg, trying to free it, but only succeeded in causing a jolt of pain to shoot up it instead. The intruder was muttering something, and I was sure a spell was being cast against me. I felt around for my wand and grabbed it, quickly casting a shield spell. It worked; the intruder stopped speaking and as far as I was aware, everything was still normal.

"Rhea, goddess mother, free my leg," I muttered, and an instant later I managed to release my foot from under the fridge and scramble to my feet.

Now I just had this intruder to contend with. A magic fight where both participants were invisible was not exactly ideal, but it was what I had to deal with.

CHAPTER 18

"*R*hea, mother of the gods, reveal this witch or wizard," I shouted, pointing my wand around the room. I figured if I could see the person I was up against, I'd have a better shot of managing to stop them before they got me. Unfortunately, nothing happened. They must have cast a protection spell around themselves, like I'd done.

This was ridiculous. If whoever was there was protected from magic, there was only one way to defeat them: without magic.

I listened for the other witch or wizard's footsteps. I heard them a minute later, and I charged.

My shoulder connected with something and I heard a squeal, and a cry of "oh no, my wand!" as the intruder and I crashed to the floor. There was something familiar about the voice.

At the same time, there came a cry from the other

142 | SAMANTHA SILVER

room. What on earth was going on? This was ridiculous.

"*Rhea, mother of the gods, cancel out all spells cast in your name,*" I called out, waving my wand around the room. It meant that Willow and I would become visible again, but at least we'd know who we were up against.

I found myself staring right into the face of Grandma Rosie.

"Seriously?" I said, scrambling to my feet to help my grandmother up. "What on earth are you doing here?"

"I could ask you the same question," Grandma Rosie said, carefully straightening out her clothes. She was dressed in a bright purple tracksuit that would have been popular back in the eighties. I was half expecting her to be holding a couple of one-pound weights in each hand. Was this seriously the disguise she was going with? What kind of senior citizen goes for their evening stroll in the middle of the night?

"Willow? Are you ok?" I called out, looking into the living room, where I found my friend helping Connie up off the ground.

"I'm fine," she said. "Is that your grandmother in the kitchen?"

"It certainly is," Grandma Rosie replied for me, peeking her head over my shoulder to look into the living room herself. "Now, what on earth are you doing breaking and entering into this young man's home?"

I threw up my hands. "Seriously? I could ask you the same question."

"We were looking for the bathroom and got a little bit lost," my grandmother deadpanned, and I groaned and buried my head in my hands. Was this seriously where I got it from? Was I destined to be Grandma Rosie when I grew old?

"What about you?" she continued. "Why are you here?"

"We're trying to find proof that Jason Oakland is Blaze's killer," I replied. My grandmother narrowed her eyes at me.

"I knew it. I knew this whole time you were trying to get in on my turf and sneak the reward money out from under me. I just knew it."

"I really only made the decision the other day," I said. "But after I was fired from my job, I figured I didn't really have any other good options."

"How did you figure out that Jason is the killer?" Willow asked Connie, who made her way next to Grandma Rosie.

"Like we're going to tell you anything," Grandma Rosie said quickly before Connie could answer. I rolled my eyes.

"Look, obviously we all know he's the killer. It's not like telling us how you got to that conclusion is going to change our minds."

"Then why don't you tell us how you got here," Grandma Rosie said, narrowing her eyes at me.

"Fine," I said, throwing up my hands. "We found out Jason was selling illegal potions to a bunch of dragons looking for a good time, including Blaze's sister, and Blaze was threatening Jason to get him to stop selling to Bridget."

Connie nodded. "That's what we found out, too. We haven't spoken to Bridget, but Rosie knows a couple of dragons, and that's what they told us."

"So why did you come here tonight?"

"We wanted to find traces of the poison he used before he got rid of it," Grandma Rosie said. Great minds really did think alike. Although frankly, if this was an idea Grandma Rosie came up with, I was starting to wonder if I was really on the right track.

"Ok, well, let's agree that we never saw each other and get out of here."

"If you breathe a word of what happened here tonight to your mother, you'll be sorry," Grandma Rosie said to me, grabbing me by the arm.

"Are you threatening me?" I said, pulling away. I couldn't believe my seventy-something-year-old grandmother was actually threatening me. Why couldn't I have a normal grandmother who spent her nights baking cookies, not breaking into illegal potion dealers' homes?

"I'm just letting you know how it is," she replied.

"Fine. I won't tell her if you don't tell her," I said, narrowing my eyes at Grandma Rosie. The two of us stared each other down for a second, until Willow waved a hand between our faces.

"Come on, both of you. We need to get out of here before Jason gets home."

"You two can leave. Connie and I haven't had a look around yet."

"Fine," I said. "We're going."

I grabbed Willow by the wrist and the two of us left the apartment.

"What if he comes back while they're still there?" Willow asked, looking back toward Jason's place as we walked briskly back to the park.

"Not our problem," I replied firmly. "Besides, those two old ladies can take care of themselves. And if they get locked up in jail when they get caught breaking into a second place in less than twenty-four hours, well, I guess the reward money will have to go toward their bail."

Willow laughed. "Well, let's see if we can figure out what these potions are made of and get back to your place before we get caught out here and arrested instead."

"Wouldn't Grandma Rosie just find that to be the biggest hoot," I muttered as Willow and I made our way back to my place. As we entered, I pulled the vials out from my pocket and set them down on the table. Vials were always magically enhanced to make them unbreakable, so even though they were made of glass, they had come through our entire adventure completely unscathed.

Willow and I looked at the samples carefully now that we were no longer at risk of being caught.

The first potion, which had been in the biggest cauldron, was a dark rust color. It looked thick and grainy, and frankly, not at all appetizing. The one next to it, on the other hand, was blue with swirls of silver, like a flowing river in the moonlight.

"I hope that one's ok to take," I said, motioning toward it, and Willow gave me a you-know-better-than-that look.

"Really? You want to be able to drink a random potion we found in *that* apartment because it looks pretty?"

"The pretty ones shouldn't be poisonous. It's not fair."

"That's exactly how nature works. The bright colors are supposed to tell you to stay away. It's too bad you were born with the instincts of a suicidal bird. You'd be the first one trying to eat the poisonous butterfly."

"What can I say, at least I'd die with a full stomach," I said with a shrug, turning my attention to the last two vials. One was a rather dark shade of green, with foam on the top, and the last one was a canary yellow color that reminded me of a fresh can of paint.

"Do you have any poison testing strips here?" Willow asked, and I nodded.

"Yeah, of course." Every good earth coven witch owned poison testing strips. Potions were an essential part of our lives, and we had to make sure when we made new or complicated potions that we weren't going to risk our lives by drinking them, plus be able to check potions of unknown provenance.

Why Jason Oakland didn't bother with these precautions when he made his was absolutely beyond me. He was probably too lazy to check, or too concerned with how it would affect his bottom line to worry about it.

I pulled out two strips and handed them to Willow, then took another two myself. I placed them in the two vials closest to me, with half the strip inserted into the potion and the other half sticking out. If the strips turned red, that meant they were poisonous. If they turned green, we were good to go.

I was so intently focused on the strips, convinced one of them was going to go red, that when they all turned green, I groaned.

"Oh, come on," I said. "Maybe we should try again."

Willow gave me one of her looks. "Really? You think the *magic* might be wrong?"

"Fine," I admitted. "None of these are poisonous. I was seriously hoping one of them would be, though. It would have proven that Jason was our killer. Now we're just going to have to find some other kind of proof, since there wasn't any in his home."

"Right. I managed to check the living room, bedroom, and bathroom before we left. There was nothing there."

I frowned. "He's not that smart. There has to be a way to prove it was him."

"Well, if we're going to brainstorm for a while, I want some hot chocolate," Willow said.

"Oooh, good idea," I replied, going to the kitchen. After all, it had been quite cold out, and even though the adrenaline was still pumping through my veins, I knew it would soon be replaced by a seeping cold. Making my way to the kitchen, I warmed some milk in a cauldron before adding some chocolate from a pack I'd gotten as a gift from Leda for my birthday a few weeks back. The chocolate came from a company in Pacific Cove called Phoenix Chocolates, and I was very excited to try it. Apparently, the chocolate in their hot chocolate mixes came straight from Belgium; this definitely promised to be a good hot chocolate experience.

The drinks didn't disappoint. I figured Willow and I had earned a little bit of luxury after our experience that night, so when it was ready, I poured the hot chocolate into a couple of mugs and topped them both off with generous cones of whipped cream.

I handed Willow her mug and sat down next to her on the couch. I took a deep sip of the drink.

"Well, I think I got tonight's events wrong," I said. "Obviously, Grandma Rosie killed me and I went to heaven, because there's no way anything on earth should possibly taste as good as this hot chocolate."

"I know, right?" Willow replied, looking at me with

a stupefied expression. "It's so good. Where did you get it?"

"Leda got it for me as a gift from a company in Pacific Cove. Phoenix Chocolates."

"Oh, I've heard of them. The owner is the daughter of the owners of Pacific Cove Chocolates, the couple that got arrested a few months back."

"For making chocolate so good it's actually illegal?"

"Fraud, or embezzlement, or something."

"Well, that's a bit of a bummer. But yeah, this hot chocolate is amazing."

We sipped in silence for a bit, savoring the taste of our delicious drinks, before moving the conversation back to Jason and how I was going to *prove* that he had killed Blaze.

"What if Grandma Rosie and Connie manage to find something we missed?" I asked.

"Then we move on. If they find the proof, they find the proof. You can't worry about them—you can only think about doing the best *you* can," Willow replied, and I nodded. That made sense. All I could do was the best I could; I couldn't worry about anyone else.

I flopped down on the couch, exhaustion suddenly overtaking me. "Ugh. I need to find that proof."

"Why don't you focus on getting a good night's sleep first? After all, if your brain isn't rested, it won't be able to find any proof, either."

"Gee, thanks, Mom," I teased as Willow got up and

put a Sherpa blanket over me. I snuggled deep into it as Willow turned off the lights.

"I'm going home now; I have to work in the morning too."

"Thanks for everything," I mumbled with my eyes closed. "You're the best."

I could feel Willow smiling at me as she closed the door behind her and left. I didn't even have the energy to crawl over to my bed in the other room; I woke up the next morning still lying on the couch, one arm hanging off the edge and onto the floor, the side of my face pressed into the pillow.

CHAPTER 19

*A*fter making my way to the kitchen as the memories of last night flooded back to me, I put a pot of coffee on before dragging myself to the bathroom for a shower that might blast me awake. When I stepped out of it ten minutes later, I began to feel vaguely human again, drying my hair with a quick spell before making my way back to the kitchen where the aroma of drip coffee reached my nostrils.

"This is definitely going to be a three cup kind of day," I muttered to myself as I poured a mug and added a spoonful of sugar. I was leaning against the counter, enjoying the first sip of my coffee, when my phone buzzed, indicating I had a text.

Grabbing it, I saw the text was from Willow.

Anne didn't show up for her studies today. The other students don't know where she is. Did she say anything to you?

I frowned as I thought back to the conversation I'd had with Anne the day before. I sent back a quick reply. *No, nothing.*

I hoped everything was ok. Given the state she seemed to be in, I imagined she would have just taken a mental health day and not thought to give anybody a heads-up, but I made a note to stop in at her place later on today if I could find out where she lived just to check in on her.

As for myself, I didn't really have all that much to do. I let out an involuntary yawn—it appeared that one cup of coffee wasn't going to be enough to get me through this day—and then considered my options. I didn't want to spend yet another day lazing around doing nothing while I hoped proof of Jason's wrong-doing would just drop into my lap. But at the same time, I also didn't really know exactly where I was going with this. What was the next step? Should I follow Jason around to see if he went back to the scene of the crime? Maybe I should have checked the knives in his kitchen to see if they matched those of Blaze's killer. Did I have to break into his home again? Would I be interrupted by my own grandmother once more if I tried?

I wondered if Grandma Rosie and Connie got back safely last night, but then I hadn't gotten a panicked visit from my mother yet this morning, so I assumed she was none the wiser about her mother's extra-curricular activities.

Eventually I decided on the tried-and-true method for gathering information and gossip in any small town: checking out the coffee shop. Besides, I was going to have to find out where Anne lived somehow if I wanted to check in on her, and that was also the best way to go.

The fact that I'd be able to eat some scrumptious potion-enhanced goodies to give me the energy to get through the day was just an added bonus.

I slipped on some clothes, checked in the bathroom mirror to confirm I looked more or less presentable—I was erring on the side of "less," but close enough—and slipped out the front door, stifling yet another yawn.

I inched past my mother's house, daring a glance through the kitchen window to see her and Grandma Rosie sitting at the table drinking tea together. It didn't look like my mom had tried to murder my grand-mother recently, so I figured Grandma Rosie must have gotten in and out last night without my mom finding out. It was good to see she wasn't in jail, at least.

Making my way down to The Magic Brewmstick, I turned over everything I knew in my head. How was I going to find proof Jason was the killer? Or was I looking at it all wrong?

I sighed and made my way into the building. I was pleased to see the fairy working the counter this morning was Pyxis. She had worked at The Magic Brewmstick for as long as I could remember, at least ten years, and she was hands down the biggest gossip in town. The problem was, only about one quarter of the things she said at any given moment were actually true, and so whenever one was dealing with Pyxis, the trouble was figuring out if what she was telling you was accurate or completely made up.

"Hi, Pyxis," I greeted her with a smile. "How are things?"

"Well, if it isn't Althea Everwood," Pyxis replied. "How can I help the granddaughter of Mt. Rheanier's most notorious criminal today?"

I smiled. "I'm guessing you heard about my grand-mother being caught in the Enforcers' office the other day?"

Pyxis shot me a wink. Her light brown curls bobbed up and down slightly as her silver wings fluttered excitedly behind her. "Oh, honey, it's the only thing anyone was talking about yesterday. Well, apart from the murder," she added in a conspiratorial whisper, as if the murder of one of the town's citizens was a secret between the two of us. I resisted the urge to roll my eyes.

"Have you heard anything else?" I asked. "I've heard a rumor that he was killed by Jason."

"Oh, no, no," Pyxis replied, shaking her head so her curls bounced around her face. "No, that's not right at all. I have it from a very good source that he killed himself."

My eyebrows rose. "Is that right?"

Pyxis's nod was vigorous. "Or at least, that's what *they* want you to think."

"Who's they?"

"The group of rich dragons who killed him so that they could take over the parents' inheritance when they died. After all, he was enormously rich, you know."

"Well, if those dragons are already rich, why would they need more money?"

"Because rich people always want more. That's what they do. Even if it involves murder."

"Well, then what about Bridget, Blaze's sister? Why wasn't she killed?"

Pyxis looked at me sympathetically, as if she felt bad about the fact that I hadn't figured out the truth yet.

"Honey, you can't do two fake suicides at the same time. If you're going to kill two people at once, you have to make it look like an accident, like they were riding the same broom and fell off, or something. I don't even know how that would work with dragons. But they're obviously going to wait before they kill her. She hasn't been in yet, which is a shame. I hope I get to speak to her and tell her to be careful."

"Right," I said. "Well, thanks for the chat, Pyxis. It's been…enlightening, as always."

"Oh, no problem. If you want to know anything else about the town's happenings, let me know. But anyway, what can I get for you today?"

I ordered a coffee and a donut with an energy-boosting crème center, then made my way to the long wooden table in the middle of the room that acted as a de facto town watercooler. It was well-known that if you wanted privacy, you stuck to the tables against the walls or the patio outside. If you were at the big table, that meant you were fair game to talk.

Plonking myself down, I immediately took a bite of the donut and straightaway felt energy beginning to course through me. Much better. A couple of fairies were sitting at the far end of the table, one with gorgeous blonde hair that reached her hips, and the other with a short, black pixie cut that framed her face beautifully. I knew them—I was fairly certain they worked checkout at the grocery store—but we certainly weren't friends or anything.

"Your grandmother got caught breaking into the Enforcers' office the other day, didn't she?" the blonde one said to me immediately. "That must have been quite something."

"Yes, well, Grandma Rosie has been losing her marbles a little bit the last few years," I lied. If only I had the excuse that my grandmother wasn't completely sane when she *broke into an Enforcers' office*.

Of course, I supposed I couldn't really throw all that many stones from inside my glass house.

"Such a shame," the brunette sighed, shaking her head. "I always liked your grandmother. When I was little, she once caught me trying to steal candy from the convenience store. Instead of turning me in, she distracted the clerk so I could get away."

I laughed. "That sounds about right." Helping random children commit petty theft was definitely the sort of thing my grandmother would have done.

"She was trying to find evidence of Blaze's killer, though, wasn't she?" the blonde asked, more seriously this time. "I can't believe how many people are trying to find the killer themselves, thanks to the reward."

"I think she is, but you'd have to ask her," I said. I didn't really want to lie, but I also didn't want to give away all of Grandma Rosie's secrets. "Who else is trying to solve it?"

"Well, there's a witch named Andrea doing it," the blonde fairy replied. "I saw her the other day, bothering Chief Enforcer Loeb. The Chief Enforcer didn't look happy."

I smiled. "I can imagine it's been rough for her."

"I think her patience is wearing thin. I heard three werewolf shifters were arrested in town the other night, too. They were stalking around, looking for people acting suspiciously. And then there was a witch who was caught trying to sneak over on a broom to the lookout where he was found. The dragon shifter guarding the lookout had to shift into a dragon to catch her."

I shook my head. "That's insane. I haven't heard of any of that."

"I know Chief Enforcer Loeb wants to keep it on

the down low," the brunette said. "She's worried that if people find out about this, all it's going to do is cause more people to try and solve the case themselves. But you know how word gets around."

"I do," I smiled.

"But the thing is, no one really knows who could have done it. I mean, it's Blaze we're talking about! If ever there was a shifter who didn't get into a single spot of trouble in his life, it's him."

"I've heard a few people talking about how he got into an argument with a wizard, but I'm not sure who," I said.

"Oh, yeah, Jason Oakland," the blonde fairy replied. "We heard about that as well. Apparently some people were scoping out his place the other day, but they got away before the Enforcers got there."

"Oh?" I said, my eyebrows rising. I couldn't help but wonder if that was the night my grandmother got herself covered in paint.

"Apparently Pyxis saw him walking down the street by himself the morning Blaze was killed, though," the blonde added. "So most people have moved on from that theory. At least from what I've heard."

My head spun to the counter where the fairy was leaning in toward someone, obviously giving them some more top-secret information. Was it true? Had she really seen Jason right around the time of the murder? If so, that meant he was innocent. But he couldn't be innocent. Everything pointed to him.

And at the same time, Pyxis was the least trust-worthy fairy in town. I mean, sure, when her gossip was good, it was excellent. But it was also wrong more often than not.

I couldn't help but wonder.

"Anyway, we have to go to work," the fairies said to me. I said goodbye to them, rather distractedly, my mind elsewhere.

Then another thought struck me. What if the fairies were lying to me? After all, they'd just finished telling me all about how multiple paranormals were trying to solve the murder. What if they were two of them, and they figured I was their competition?

I decided to get the info straight from the source. When Pyxis found herself free again, I went up to see her.

"Hello, honey, looking for a refill on that coffee?"

"Not yet, although I might get a second donut," I said, thinking about how little money I had left and how spending a good chunk of my current net worth on a donut probably wasn't the smartest play. I ended up justifying it by telling myself it would be worth it if the extra energy kicked my brain into gear and I found the proof I was after.

Was I counting my chickens before they hatched? Definitely. But I was also very much craving that second donut.

"Did you see Jason Oakland the morning of the murder?" I asked Pyxis as she came back with my donut on a plate a second later. I tried sounding casual about it, but I was pretty sure I'd failed.

"I did," Pyxis replied, her eyes widening. "It was that morning, just before nine."

Yup, that fit in with my timeframe for the murder. "Are you sure about the time?"

"Absolutely. My shift here started at nine, and I was on my way. I walked through the door here at 8:55, about two minutes after I spotted Jason."

"So he was here, in town?"

"Just down the street," Pyxis confirmed. "Walking, muttering to himself, looking completely out of it. I thought he was high, to be honest, but it wasn't even nine in the morning. A bit early to have taken some of your own potions."

"Yeah," I said to myself, deep in thought. If Pyxis was telling the truth, did that mean Jason was innocent? Or did she have the time wrong? Or maybe Jason flew to meet Blaze at the outlook a few minutes after Pyxis saw him.

"Did he have a broom with him at the time?" I asked, and Pyxis nodded.

"Sure. He did, yeah. Just a normal-looking one. I remembered thinking I should call the Enforcers; there was no way he was in a state to fly, but then he *was* only walking around, not flying, so I supposed there was nothing they could have done."

"Thanks," I said. Then another thought popped into

my head. "You wouldn't happen to know where the witch Anne Leavis lives, would you?"

"Of course. She lives in the small block of apartments behind the grocery store. She shares a two-bedroom apartment with some of the other assistant Healer students."

"Thanks," I said, taking the donut. I scarfed it down quickly and then made my way back outside, heading toward the grocery store.

CHAPTER 20

I looked up at the ominous-looking sky as I walked along, wondering if I was going to have to pull out my wand to cast an umbrella spell on myself sooner rather than later. I loved fall, but regular torrential downpours were a fact of life during this time of year in the Pacific Northwest, and the dark gray clouds above certainly looked like they were ready to open up any minute.

Picking up the pace a bit, I made my way toward the grocery store. It was on the outskirts of town, closer to the woods, and I knew the apartment building Pyxis meant. It was an older building with cheap rent, the sort of place that was perpetually inhabited by young paranormals who wanted to leave home but didn't have careers that could afford them a nicer place.

I hoped to be able to afford a place in there so I

could move out of the adapted shed I was currently living in sooner rather than later.

It wasn't really the shed that was the issue. The shed was fine. Small, but fine. It was more the proximity to my family that I was opposed to.

As I approached the building, I furrowed my brow slightly. There were more people around here than I had expected; what was going on? It was the middle of the morning, not exactly grocery store rush hour, and most people weren't heading toward the store—they were making their way to the same building I was.

"What's going on?" I asked a witch that I vaguely recognized from around.

"Apparently there's been a murder in that building," the witch replied in a hushed voice. "At least, that's what I heard. The Enforcers are there and everything!"

I pushed through the growing crowd until I reached the red-and-yellow police cordon emblazoned with the town's logo and the words "crime scene—do not enter." I already knew it was magically enhanced so that no one unauthorized could get past it, so I didn't even bother trying.

Instead, I absorbed the scene as best I could. Sure enough, the entire building had been cordoned off and declared a crime scene. Looking through the lobby, I could see a few witches, including one that I recognized as having walked out just ahead of Anne the other day, huddled together. They looked like they were crying.

My heart dropped. Anne wasn't among them. Was she ok?

My eyes scanned the area, looking for any sign of Anne. Eventually, they settled on Jack. He was speaking with Chief Enforcer Loeb. If she was here, that meant whatever had happened here was serious.

I sent Willow a text, asking if they'd heard anything at the hospital, but she responded in the negative. She did add that she'd been busy all morning dealing with the aftermath of a firefight between two dragon shifters, though, and likely wouldn't have heard any news.

My eyes followed Jack as he left Chief Enforcer Loeb and made his way toward the back of the building. I followed the cordoned-off perimeter until finally I was close enough to be within earshot of him.

"Jack," I called out as loudly as I dared, not wanting to attract the attention of any of the looky-loos near the front of the building. He spun around, spotted me, and came over briskly.

"What's going on?" he asked.

"I was going to ask you the same thing. Anne Leavis. Is she ok?"

Jack gave me a hard look. "She's dead."

"What?"

"Yeah. How do you know her?"

I pressed my lips together, and Jack put a hand on his hip.

"You do realize this is a murder investigation?"

"She was killed?"

"Yes. Around five this morning. Her two room-mates had spent the night at a friend's house to study. They came back during their mid-morning break about forty minutes ago to grab some food and get changed when they found the body. We're trying to keep that information quiet for now."

"It's not working; one of the witches already told me someone was murdered. I didn't know if she was right, though."

Jack sighed. "Sometimes I hate small towns."

"What happened to her?" Jack gave me a look. "Oh, come on, this way I don't have to break into the office and find out myself."

"You know, there is a middle ground that involves you going on with your life without pestering me *or* committing any crimes."

"There really isn't," I replied, crossing my arms. Jack looked at me and sighed.

"Fine, but only because you would be the most annoying inmate ever if they locked you up in our holding cell."

I grinned. "Thanks."

"But you have to tell me how you know Anne Leavis first."

I considered it for a moment, then nodded. "She was dating Blaze," I replied. "They were keeping their relationship a secret, since his parents are super old-

166 | SAMANTHA SILVER

fashioned and didn't want him dating anyone who wasn't a shifter."

"Ok. She told us that when we spoke to her after finding that text. Do you have any reason to think she might have killed Blaze?"

I shrugged. "No, not really. I mean, there was that text she sent him. I assume you saw it?"

Jack nodded. "Yeah. She seemed really confused about it."

"Same here. I believe her."

"Between us, so do I."

"Willow doesn't, though. She thinks it might have been Anne. I guess not."

Jack sighed. "Honestly, I wish this case would get solved. Do you know how many people have tried to break into Jason Oakland's house this week? At least four, that I know of. On the bright side, only you and your grandmother were stupid enough to break into the Enforcers' office. But this reward money has everyone fighting each other for a piece of it, and I'm sick and tired of it. I wish the family would recall the reward and just let us do our job. Maybe then Anne Leavis would still be alive."

"How was she killed?" I asked.

"Strangled. Don't tell anyone that."

"You know I won't."

Jack sighed. "Only because it's going to help you try and find the killer you're after."

"I don't get it," I said. "I'm sure Jason is the killer,

but he wouldn't even have known about Anne. There's literally no way. They kept their relationship completely secret."

"You still think Jason is the killer?" Jack asked, and I shrugged.

"Everything about it makes sense. Everything except that one text. He had the means, he had the motive, he had the opportunity. Even if he was in town just before nine the morning Blaze was killed, he had a broom with him. He could have flown to the lookout. But the text message doesn't fit. I don't know how he sent the text."

Jack looked at me, nodding slowly. I felt like he was holding something back. "What is it?"

"Nothing," he said, shaking his head.

"Are you close to making an arrest?" I asked, and Jack shrugged.

"It's not up to me. And you know I can't tell you that."

"Do you think Jason is the killer?"

"I genuinely don't know. I don't like to jump to conclusions without having all of the facts. I will say, if Anne's death and Blaze's death are linked, the key to solving this case will be finding out who knew about their relationship."

Jack was right. They had to be linked. There was no way someone would randomly kill Anne a few days after killing Blaze. Not in a place like Mt. Rheanier, where murders were virtually unheard of.

There was no way this was a coincidence. Absolutely none.

But if that was the case, I had a different problem: what reason could Jason possibly have to kill Anne Leavis?

"Fine," I said. "Keep your secrets."

"That's sort of my job," Jack replied.

"Yeah, well, your job is stupid." My mind raced with thoughts; I didn't have time to be either mature or clever. Besides, now that I'd gotten the information I needed, I was back to being mad at Jack.

"It was lovely helping you out, too. Anyway, I have to go."

I watched Jack's retreating form as I turned over all of this new information in my head.

Who knew that Blaze and Anne had been seeing each other? That was the key here.

CHAPTER 21

I needed to speak to the assistant Healer students that Anne lived with, but I also needed to speak with Jason Oakland. And fast. I wanted to get to him before anyone else did, and it sounded like there were a lot of people on that track.

I raced down to his building and began pounding on his door.

"Hold on, hold on," I heard him mutter. He opened the door a moment later, bleary-eyed, wearing only a pair of boxers. The dude looked like death. His skin was pale, his breathing was ragged, and I wasn't even completely sure he recognized me.

"Hey, what's up, pretty witch?" he said, leaning casually against the doorframe. Seriously? The guy was trying to flirt with me? He looked like he needed to be begging me to call an ambulance, not trying to get me to bed.

"I need some answers, idiot," I said, pushing him backward and storming into his apartment.

"Woah, hey," he said slowly, as if it took his brain a few seconds to catch up to the rest of him. "What's going on? Who are you?"

"Did you know Blaze was dating Anne Leavis?"

"Woah. Wait, what?"

I rolled my eyes and went to the kitchen, popping open cupboards until I found a box of instant coffee. I cast a quick spell, poured some boiling water into a mug, and dropped in the instant coffee, stirring it with a dirty-looking spoon that still looked cleaner than most of the stuff in this apartment.

I was going to have to take a shower in bleach after touching this stuff. I pushed the mug toward Jason. "Drink."

He obeyed, taking the mug from me and sipping the coffee. "You're insane. What are you doing in my apartment?"

"Trying to get answers. I'll try again. Did you know Anne Leavis was dating Blaze?"

"I don't know Anne Leavis, but she's a witch, right? I know some of the Leavis family," Jason replied. "No, I didn't know she was dating the dragon. I had no idea. Why were they dating? They were different species."

"It's 2019, that sort of thing happens now. But so you genuinely had no idea they were dating?"

"What would I know? All I know is that dirtbag of a

dragon wanted me to stop selling my stuff. It's like he doesn't care about my livelihood at all."

I narrowed my eyes at him. "I heard you got a job working at Magical Pharmaceuticals."

"Yeah, well, they fired me after I mixed up silver-weed and white hemstail. Who on earth can tell the difference between those, anyway? They claimed I ruined an entire batch of potion. Who cares? Now that Blaze is dead, I can keep making money my way, anyway."

I had to hide the smile that threatened to appear; I was glad Jason had ruined an entire batch of potions for that company. It served them right.

"So now that Blaze is dead you're dealing again. And apparently sampling the merchandise, too."

"Hey, gotta make sure it's alright to take."

No wonder dragons were ending up in the hospital. If I cared a little bit more about Jason, I probably would have dragged him over there myself. He looked like he was going to keel over and die any second.

"Where were you this morning at around five?"

"Uhhhh...sleeping? Making potions? Honestly, I'm not really sure," he said, scratching the side of his head. "Sorry."

Great. That was about as solid an alibi as he had for Blaze's murder. I was starting to get sick and tired of this guy.

"Do you have any poisonous potion in here?" I asked. After all, if he really was high right now, there was a chance he'd answer me and solve all my problems.

"Nah. I'd never mess with that stuff. I'm all about good times. And speaking of good times…"

"Ugh, not on your life," I said, scrunching up my face as Jason looked toward the bedroom. "Gross."

"Hey, you could have left it at no. You didn't have to insult me."

"You insulted me just by offering," I shot back. "Anyway, I think that's my cue to leave." I didn't think I was going to get any more information out of Jason. And I wanted to get to the hospital. I needed to speak to Willow, and hopefully the friend that Anne's room-mates had spent the night with.

As I left Jason's apartment, I ran into Grandma Rosie and Connie making their way down the street. My eyes narrowed. "You're not getting into any more trouble, are you?"

"Who, us?" my grandmother replied, doing her best to look as innocent as possible. "Wouldn't dream of it. How dare you accuse your grandmother of such a thing?"

"Right," I replied with an eye roll. "I forgot, you're a sweet little thing who wouldn't dream of causing any sort of mischief."

"That's right, and don't you forget it," Grandma Rosie said, wagging a finger at me. I looked past her at Connie, who was now standing with her feet spread apart and her arms crossed, like a five-foot-two-inch bodyguard with big white curls.

"Where are you going, anyway? If you want to bug Jason, he's currently super high, so there's no point."

"Right, like you'd tell us the truth," Grandma Rosie replied. "We're looking for information. Can't let ourselves get distracted by the other murder. That one's far less promising; I know Anne Leavis's family, and they don't have any money to put up a reward."

I smiled to myself; Grandma Rosie and Connie didn't realize there was a link between Blaze and Anne. At least this meant I was one step ahead of them.

"Is that your only motivation to stop a murderer? Money?" I asked.

"Well, I must admit, it has been a good way to get out of the house. And my Healer *has* been telling me I need to stay active in my twilight years."

"I'm not sure committing crimes while trying to catch a murderer is exactly what he had in mind."

"Well, he should have been more specific, then."

"Alright, well, I'll leave you to it," I said. I had to make my way to the hospital. I wanted to speak to the assistant Healers before anyone else got there, but as I walked off, I realized Grandma Rosie and Connie actually had the same thought as everyone else investigating this crime would: that the murders of Anne Leavis and Blaze were completely unrelated.

On the bright side, that meant I wasn't going to

have to push my way through hordes of paranormals trying to bother grieving witches and wizards.

I texted Willow as soon as I arrived at the hospital and she met me in the cafeteria, where I grabbed the only thing I could afford—a cup of free water from the cooler next to the cutlery stand.

Her hair stood on end and she looked like she could use a coffee—or ten.

"I heard about Anne," she said as soon as she plonked herself down. "It's just awful. What an awful day."

"I'm sorry," I said, reaching a hand across the table and placing it on top of Willow's. She gave me a weak smile. "It sounds like today's not been great."

"It's been straight-up awful. Those dragons are going to be scarred for life. What kind of idiots decide to play chicken with flaming fire breath? We've got assistant Healers creating salve potions right now, and if it weren't for what happened, we'd have all the students out getting ingredients for more. The strongest potion we have requires a bunch of fresh basil, fresh silverweed, and fresh rose petals. We don't have the supplies to make enough."

"I'll do it," I immediately replied. "I know where the basil and silverweed are. You'll have to send someone else to go buy rose petals somewhere they're still in bloom, since it's too late in the season here, as you know, but I can take care of the other two. I'll get as much as you need."

Willow shot me the world's most grateful look. "Are you sure?"

"Of course. I don't want any of the assistant Healers to have to go out and work, not after the news they've just gotten. Heck, *I'm* saddened about her death. I can't imagine how the students who worked side by side with her every single day are coping."

There wasn't a doubt in my mind that this was the right thing to do. The chat I wanted to have with the student the roommates had spent the night with could wait. This was more important. If the hospital needed supplies for potions, I'd much rather it be me sent out to do it.

"Can you do it now? I'll let the hospital administrator and the Healer in charge of the dragons know."

"Yeah," I replied, getting up. It was a good thing I'd eaten that second donut after all. "How much do you need?"

"Literally as much as you can get. Of both. The dragons are going to need the salve put all over themselves for the next few weeks. We're probably going to have to get some extra supplies from elsewhere, but for now, we're just trying to keep up with the demand while not having any assistant Healer students to use for help."

"Got it," I nodded. I immediately made my way back home, grabbed my bag for collecting plants, and made my way back outside. I pursed my lips as I looked at the broom. This sort of situation was urgent; I had heard from Willow that the strongest burn salve—the one I assumed these ingredients were for—had to sit for six hours before it was ready to be used. Time would definitely be of the essence if they were running out.

But I really didn't enjoy flying.

Still, it was important. I sighed, grabbed the broom, and hopped onto it. Soaring up into the sky, I pushed down the wave of anxiety I usually felt when I started flying and made my way toward the lookout. There was definitely no time to admire the view today. Besides, it wasn't as nice when the clouds were overcast and so low I felt like I was about to hit the ceiling as I flew upward.

If there was one thing I *definitely* hated, it was flying in clouds. I always lost all sense of direction and usually ended up upside down when I did it.

Swooping over toward the lookout, I kept an eye out for the Enforcer guarding the place and was surprised to see a familiar face.

CHAPTER 22

"*A*ndy?" I called out, and the wizard spun around to face me.

"Oh, hey, you're Ali, right?" he said in his Australian drawl, and I nodded.

"Sorry, you're not allowed here," he continued. "This part of town is currently out of bounds until the investigation into Blaze's death is concluded."

"I know," I rushed. "I'm not here to see the crime scene. There's a basil field not far from here, and I need to get to it."

Andy looked at me skeptically. "Jack told me to watch out for you, that if anyone in town was likely to lie to me to get around the law, it would be you…or your grandmother."

"Wait," I said, suddenly realizing there was some-thing wrong with this picture. "You're an Enforcer?"

"That's right. Chief Enforcer Loeb thought there

was need for a second wizard to be brought in to beef up security after the break-ins at the offices, and I was looking for a change of scenery. Plus, there aren't all that many Enforcers' offices that are happy to have wizards on board. Chief Enforcer Loeb is an outlier for sure."

"So you're not gay." There went my mouth again, speaking before my brain had time to tell it what a terrible idea that was.

Andy laughed good-naturedly. "I'm afraid not."

"Good," I replied, immediately clamping a hand to my mouth. Andrew raised an eyebrow. "I don't mean 'good' in that I think there's anything wrong with that," I quickly added. But I didn't know where to go from there. How did I explain that I meant "good" as in I wanted to be all over him, without letting him know in any way that I wanted to be all over him?

How on earth did I get myself into these situations?

Luckily, Andy waved away my embarrassment with a cheeky grin. "Wait, when you saw me with Jack the other day, did you think we were together?"

"Yeah," I admitted with a shrug.

"Well, I'll take that as a compliment. I'm secure enough in my masculinity that I can admit he's hot as anything, but I fall firmly on the female side of things when it comes to partners."

"I'm straight too," I replied, just in case I hadn't embarrassed myself enough already. Seriously? There was basically a zero percent chance at this point of

Andy thinking of me as anything other than an idiot. He smiled at me, and I couldn't help but feel it was the sort of smile you gave to the kid eating glue while all the others were busy making papier-mâché.

"Well, now that we've got that out of the way, you said you were here for some basil?"

I winced inwardly. Great, he was turning the conversation back to business. That meant he really did think I was an idiot. "That's right," I nodded. "You've probably heard about the murder of Anne Leavis?"

Andy nodded gravely. "I have, yes. It's a tragedy."

"Yeah. She was studying to be an assistant Healer, so they've given the students the rest of the day off, but they need someone to collect a bunch of herbs to make a salve for two idiot dragons that decided to attack each other last night."

"I heard about that, too," Andy said. "Apparently their burns are intense and they're both lucky to be alive."

"That's right. But because the assistant Healer students aren't in today, I need to get some herbs for the salves, and the wild basil is one of them."

"And you said the field isn't far from here?"

"Literally less than a hundred feet."

"Well, in that case, let me come with you," Andy said. "I'll cast a ward to let me know if anyone comes close to the crime scene, and I can help you pick anything you need."

An involuntary blush crawled up my face. No, he was probably just keeping a close eye on me, since Jack had warned him about me. It was nothing more than that.

"Sure," I said, not trusting myself to say more. "The field is just over here."

I led Andy away from the lookout, overhearing him mutter a quick spell to cover the area while he was with me. It took us less than a minute to reach the basil field.

"You were right, this is close," he said. "Any specific way to do this? Sorry, I'm not great with potions." The awkward smile he shot me hit me right in the heart.

"The bigger the leaves, the better," I replied. "That's about all you need to know. Avoid the ones that are so old they have black spots on them. Put everything you've collected in this container."

The two of us started working in silence. On my part, it was because I didn't trust anything that came out of my mouth. Andy probably already thought I had the IQ of potato; I didn't want to make things worse. For him, I was fairly certain he was simply getting used to the plant collection. He seemed to study every leaf, like he wasn't sure what ones were good and what ones weren't. Non-earth coven witches and wizards were strange like that. Picking herbs was second nature for us.

Eventually, however, Andy seemed to get the gist of it and became more talkative.

"So you've lived in Mt. Rheanier your whole life? How do you like it?"

"I love it here," I replied. "Honestly, there's nowhere in the world I'd rather be. I love the mountains, I love being in the outdoors, I love the weather. Yes, even the weather."

Andy laughed. "That part's going to take me a little bit longer to get used to. While it does get cold in the southern parts of Australia in the winter, I'm from further north, where it's fairly hot year-round."

"So I guess you think this is absolutely freezing," I grinned.

"You're not wrong there. You'll find me all rugged up in the middle of summer while everyone else is wearing shorts. I do have to say though, the scenery here is gorgeous."

I nodded. "It's what I love the most about this place. I love how you can have a dip in the lake and look up at the huge mountain. I love how you can walk in the woods and become one with nature. Sometimes, especially in the morning, I look out over the lake, enjoy the view, and just think I'm the luckiest witch alive for being able to live here."

Andy smiled at me. "It's obvious you love it here. Your face lights up as soon as you start talking about Mt. Rheanier."

It was nice of him not to add that I also spoke like an actual adult witch instead of a primate who had barely evolved past drawing lines in the mud with sticks.

"I do love it," I said. "What about you? What made you want to leave Australia?"

I couldn't be sure, but I thought I saw a flash of sadness pass through Andy's eyes for a moment. He quickly replaced the pain with an easy smile. "I just wanted a bit of a change, you know? I'd lived in Australia my whole life, and I've always been the kind of person who didn't like to be tied down. So, one day, I decided I wanted to travel and make a life elsewhere. I ended up going to Europe for a bit, where I did my Enforcer training. Then it was a matter of finding somewhere looking to hire a wizard as an Enforcer, since we're not exactly in high demand, and I ended up here."

"Are you planning on staying here long? Or do you want to move on and keep traveling?"

"I haven't really decided, to be honest," Andy said. "I'm just going to play it by ear. I do want to stay here for a little while, at least. See if maybe I can find myself among nature, or something. Although I do have to say, I've never seen so many places that serve vegan food until moving here."

I grinned. "Yeah, there's a lot of those. You'd be surprised at how good vegan food can be nowadays. It's not like when I was growing up and you had the options of tofu, tofu, and slightly different tofu."

"Are you vegan?" Andy asked, and I shook my head.

"Nope. I'm afraid I love bacon and eggs too much for that. But I don't mind eating vegan from time to time."

I should ask him out. This was the perfect opportunity. But no, my mouth decided that now was a good time to stay shut.

"Anyway, I think that's about enough basil," I said instead. Really? What on earth was wrong with me? Here was a super-hot guy, an opening to ask him out on a date, and I decided to tell him we were finished with our plant collecting instead? Yeah, I had no idea why I was single.

"Ok," Andy said, standing up while I went over and looked at all the plants we'd collected. That would definitely make more than a few batches of salve.

"I still have to go get some silverweed, but that's on another side of town," I said.

"Good luck," Andy told me with a smile.

"Thanks. I'll see you around. Welcome to town." At least I wasn't just spewing out word vomit every time I opened my mouth in front of him anymore.

I knew of a decently sized patch of silverweed closer to the mountain. It would have been a decently long hike, but with the broom, it took only a few minutes. I filled up the rest of my bag with the silverweed and made my way back to the hospital.

After all, they were going to need these herbs as quickly as possible.

CHAPTER 23

$\mathcal{I}$ made my way back to the hospital and followed the signs to the burn units. A couple of Healers quickly pointed me in the right direction, and a few minutes later I found the assistant Healers in a lab room. There were at least ten cauldrons lined up on the tables, and six of them had some sort of blue smoke rising from them. The two assistant Healers were seated on chairs in the corner; one was reading a book and the other was playing on his phone.

"Are those the extra herbs?" the book reader asked, getting up, and I nodded.

"That's right. I got the basil and the silverweed. I don't have the fresh rose petals, though."

"Yes, someone else was sent to get them from the tropics, and they came by with a huge garbage bag full of them a few minutes ago. Now we can get working on more salve. Those poor dragons." She shook her head. "Luckily, they were given pain potion, so it could be worse, but my goodness, they are not going to be happy for the next week. I can't believe their fight got that bad."

The other assistant Healer shook his head. "Fledglings will be fledglings. Hopefully they'll at least learn never to do that again."

Fledglings were basically the dragon shifter equivalent of teenagers. Too many hormones, except most teenagers couldn't shoot fire at one another.

"Thanks for this," the male assistant Healer said. "We'll get right back into making more salve."

I nodded and made my way back out into the corridor. I briefly wondered if I should text Willow, but I figured she was probably hard at work.

Taking the back exit from the hospital—it was closer to home and acted as a bit of a shortcut—I passed by a crying witch. I recognized her red hair; she was one of the witches I'd seen in the lobby. She must have been one of Anne's roommates.

I briefly considered just walking past, then stopped. Surely the witch would rather I bother her now if it meant finding Anne's killer. I certainly hoped so.

"Hey," I said softly. "Are you alright?" I mean, I wanted to question her, but I wasn't a monster. I was going to make sure she was ok, first.

The witch looked up at me. Her eyes were the same shade as her hair from crying, and her cheeks were blotchy. I had never considered myself the motherly type, but I made my way over to her and took her in a big hug. I just didn't know what else to do.

"I'm sorry," I told the witch. "You were one of Anne's roommates, weren't you?"

"Yeah," the witch sobbed into my shoulder. "I can't believe she's gone. I just can't believe it."

"It's going to be ok," I told her. "I know it hurts now, but eventually it'll be ok."

"I just can't believe it. And in our home! We could have been there."

"Where did you spend the night?" I asked as casually as I could.

"We were studying at Elaine's place. It got late; we decided to crash there and go straight to class the next day. Then, when we got a break, we went home. I wanted to have a quick shower. I cast a cleaning spell on myself, but it's not quite the same, you know?"

I nodded.

"Plus, Anne hadn't shown up that morning. We just thought she slept in. She's been acting a bit strangely the last few days, so I kind of figured she was just a bit burned out. Missing one day of class wouldn't kill her."

Realizing what she'd said, the witch clasped a hand to her mouth. "I didn't mean…"

"I know," I said softly. "Who else lives with Anne?"

"It's me and Diana. We're all studying to be assistant Healers."

"Right," I said with a nod. "Did you know if Anne was seeing anyone?"

"No. She was too shy. She never seemed to be all that interested in wizards."

"Ok, thanks," I said. A part of me wanted to ask more questions, but I also didn't want to distress the witch any further. And besides, I had a sneaking suspicion she wouldn't have been able to help. She obviously didn't know that Anne had been seeing Blaze, so how could she have known who would have wanted them dead?

I stuck my head down as I walked home. I managed to step through the door approximately ten seconds before the skies opened up with a peal of thunder and began drenching the entire landscape. Raindrops pounded against my window as I looked outside.

At least now I had a few hours to think before the rain eased up. Maybe by then I would have solved the murder.

The problem was, I was completely stuck. There was no reason for Jason to have killed Anne, and there was no doubt in my mind the two murders were connected. Absolutely none.

Unfortunately, I couldn't think of anyone who would have wanted them *both* dead. No one knew they were in a relationship. They had kept it completely secret. I hadn't met anyone who had a clue they had been together.

So why were they both killed? Their lives were so different.

Willow texted me about an hour later. The rain hadn't even begun to let up.

I'm coming over. I'm bringing Thai food.

I was never going to say no to that, especially since my refrigerator's contents were looking especially sparse.

The knock on the door came a moment later, with Willow holding her wand above her, keeping the protection spell from the rain going. As soon as she stepped through the doorway, she shivered.

"It's cold out!" she announced. "Colder than October should be."

"Well, this should warm us up," I said, taking the bag from her and moving to the kitchen, where I grabbed a couple of bowls from the cupboard.

I scooped some jasmine rice into each bowl and topped it with a generous serving of the curry, then handed Willow her bowl. This was definitely perfect comfort food during a storm.

"Thanks again for the help today," Willow said. "I spoke to the assistants making the potions, and they were very grateful."

"I'm just glad I could help," I replied.

Willow shook her head. "I can't believe one of the students was killed last night. It's unbelievable."

"I'm not sure Jason did it," I replied. "The problem is, I'm completely out of suspects. I have no idea who might have wanted them both dead. No one knew they were together, and as far as I can tell, they didn't have any sort of interaction otherwise."

"Well, maybe someone is lying to you," Willow said. "Maybe someone did know about their relationship."

"Yeah, but why would anyone want to kill them for having a relationship?" I asked with a shrug. "It makes no sense. Sure, it's still a bit taboo to date outside of your own kind, but it's not worth killing people over. And it's getting more and more accepted every day."

"I don't know. You're the one trying to score half a million," Willow said with a grin. "It's up to you to figure it out, or I'm going to claim part of your fee."

"You'll have to claw it out of my cold, dead hands," I said, sticking my tongue out at her. "Hey, did you know we have a new Enforcer in town?"

"Do we really?" Willow asked, and I nodded.

"I saw him the other day. He was with Jack, bringing Grandma Rosie home."

"Oh, the Australian? Is he an Enforcer?"

"You met him, then?"

"I ran into him. He's pretty hot."

"Agreed. Although I'm also pretty sure he thinks I'm an idiot."

"Uh oh," Willow laughed. "What did you do?"

I recounted the whole story to her, which had her in stitches by the end.

"Oh, dear me," she eventually managed. "How do you get yourself into these situations? On the bright side, if you keep committing crimes, it won't be your intelligence that turns him off, it'll be your self-destructive tendencies."

"Now that's just a low blow," I replied.

"Is it? You abandoned your best friend for no reason."

"He slept with my boyfriend! I thought I was going to marry Sean!"

"Well, that obviously wasn't going to happen, was it?"

"No, but I mean, I would rather have found out more gently."

"You're the least gentle person I have ever met. You broke up with your last boyfriend via text message. I'm not saying you deserved what happened to you, because it sucked, but I am saying you should get over it and start being friends with Jack again. It's been months, and he's good for you."

"He's good for nothing," I muttered, crossing my arms.

Willow raised her eyebrows. "He let you get away with breaking into the Chief Enforcer's office."

"Only because he felt bad for me."

"Yeah, well, I think you should consider it. Why on earth a nice guy like Jack hangs out with you, I have no idea."

"It's because my snarky personality is charming," I replied. "You're too nice for me, too."

"I am, but you beat up bullies for me," Willow said with a wink as she took her bowl to the sink. "I'm going to head off. Try not to get yourself into any more trouble than usual."

I said goodbye to Willow and sat myself down on the couch. Was Willow right? Should I try and forgive Jack for what he'd done and go back to one of the best friendships I'd ever had?

Nah.

CHAPTER 24

I lay down on the couch and stared at the ceiling, tossing over everything I knew about the murder investigation in my head. What if Willow was right? What if someone else did know about the relationship between Anne and Blaze, and just wasn't letting on? That was a definite possibility. I couldn't discount that. But how was I going to find out who?

I needed to speak again with someone Blaze was close to. I needed to find Bridget.

Looking outside, I frowned. It was still absolutely pouring rain out, and the sun was going to be setting sooner rather than later. Still, if I wanted half a million abras, I couldn't be precious about the weather.

Pulling out my wand, I slipped on a jacket and cast a spell to protect me from the water. I made my way outside and grabbed my broom from next to the shed thankful for the overhang of the roof that had kept it dry.

Riding a wet broom as a witch when the rest of you was protected by an umbrella spell meant looking like you didn't have the best control of your bodily functions. It was not a good situation.

I hopped onto the broom and flew upward. I wondered if Bridget would be in the same spot I had found her the other day. That seemed to be where she liked to hide from people. If not, I could fly to the caves and see if she was there.

But sure enough, a couple of minutes later, I spotted her in the field. She had shifted and was in dragon form again, and as soon as she saw me flying overhead, she shifted back into human form. I landed to see she was soaked through to the bone.

"Do you want me to make my spell larger so it can fit you?" I asked when I landed, but she shook her head with a laugh.

"No, thanks. I'm completely drenched already anyway."

She really was; her hair was plastered to her face, her clothes clinging to her small frame.

"Not a fan of going inside?"

Bridget shook her head. "Easier to think out here."

"What are you thinking about?"

"Did you hear that Blaze's girlfriend was killed today?"

"Yes. Did you know her?"

Bridget shook her head. "No, I didn't."

"Did Kirsten know her? Mention her? They were both studying to be assistant Healers, after all."

"No. I don't think she knew her. Kirsten hung out in a small clique for the most part; Anne wasn't one of her friends."

As soon as Bridget said Anne's name, my blood went ice cold. I had never said Anne's name, and yet Bridget knew who she was. That meant Bridget had to have known about their relationship.

And all of a sudden, everything clicked. It wasn't Bridget's parents who would have been ashamed of Blaze and Anne if their relationship was made public. It was Bridget.

A smart person would have made their excuses and flown off, then told Chief Enforcer Loeb everything they'd figured out. A smart person would have gotten out of there as fast as humanly possible.

I was not a smart person.

"You killed them, didn't you?" I asked casually, and Bridget let out a humorless laugh.

"What on earth makes you think that?"

"You were ashamed of them. You found out about them somehow, didn't you? Maybe when they were at the lookout, their special spot, you flew over and saw them? After all, I saw it from my broom when I was looking for you; you would have had exactly the same view when you were flying in dragon form."

Why couldn't I just stop talking and get out of here?

What was wrong with me? Why did I see a fire and decide to throw a giant pile of gasoline on it instead of getting a firefighter?

Bridget's eyes narrowed and her spine stiffened. I was right. "Fine," she admitted. "You figured it out. How long have you known?"

"Not until you mentioned Anne's name just then. I hadn't told you her name. But it all makes sense. You got your witch friend Kirsten to make the poison, didn't you?"

"That's right," Bridget said with a grin that had no humor behind it. "She also snuck Anne's phone for a minute after causing a disruption and sent Blaze the text asking to meet at their special spot. Only, I was the one there to meet him. I pretended I was just out for a stroll, and he sat there with me. I offered him a drink from my water bottle, and he drank it. That was it. He stood up and started coughing, and when he collapsed, I pulled out a knife and stabbed him, just to be safe. Then I pushed him off the ledge and ran away as fast as I could."

"You're a monster. All because he was just dating a witch?"

"*Just* dating a witch? He was embarrassing our family. We're not just some random nobodies who can go around dating different paranormals willy-nilly. We're one of the oldest dragon shifter families in the paranormal world, and one of the richest. Do you know what kind of reputation we have to uphold? We can't have the son in the family going around dating a *witch*. That's just not acceptable."

"So you killed him," I said, crossing my arms. "Why did you have to kill her, too?"

"Because she was scum. She took advantage of my brother. She had to have only wanted him for his money, and there was no way I was letting her get a penny of it."

"How would she get any of his money if he was dead?"

"She would have blackmailed us—told us that if we didn't pay her, she would tell everyone about the relationship. Then our family's reputation would have been ruined. So she had to go. I couldn't take that risk."

"You're insane, you know that?"

Bridget scoffed at me. "What would you know? You're just a poor witch from a small coven that no one cares about."

"Yeah, and you killed your brother and his girlfriend for daring to be in love. You're literally the bad guy in every single movie ever made."

"Well, in that case, you'll understand that now that you've figured it out, I'm going to have to kill you, too."

Great. Before I had a chance to react, Bridget had shifted back into a dragon. I pointed my wand straight at her, which broke the spell that had been protecting me from the rain all this time.

Ok, so taking on a murderer directly had not been my plan when I woke up this morning. But hey, you live and learn. At least, I hoped I was about to live and learn. Bridget seemed pretty intent on preventing the former.

I cast a new shield spell, this one stronger and directly in front of me, as Bridget immediately blast fire toward me. If I hadn't been quick with my spell, I would have been the world's worst Pinterest fail.

I wanted to cast an aggressive spell to force Bridget onto her toes, but if I broke my shield spell, I would be completely unprotected. But I couldn't just stay on the defensive forever. Eventually I'd get tired, my magic would get sloppy, and I'd become one very-well-done witch. If I wanted to make it out of here alive, I was going to have to come up with a plan.

I immediately jumped up onto my broom. It wasn't that I thought I'd have an advantage in the sky; compared to a dragon, I definitely didn't. I just didn't really know what else to do. I soared up high, my shield surrounding me like a protective bubble, while Bridget roared and followed after me.

Almost instinctively, I began flying toward the top of Mt. Rheanier. The higher we got, the windier it was, and the harder it seemed for Bridget to blow fire at me accurately. This was my chance.

I cut to the left suddenly, diving below the dragon and breaking my shield spell. I pointed my wand at her and shouted.

"*Rhea, goddess mother, paralyze this dragon from head to toe.*"

Unfortunately, Bridget was nimble. Very nimble. She darted out of the way of the spell and roared fire at me once more. I didn't have the time to cast a spell, so I had to dart to the right with my broom to avoid the flames.

I looped around, finding myself behind Bridget. *"Rhea, goddess mother, put this dragon to sleep!"* I shouted. This time, the spell hit, and Bridget's eyes immediately began drooping.

She roared at me once more, but it was half-hearted, and the flame that shot out of her mouth could politely be called campfire-esque.

As I looked around, however, I realized that if Bridget fell asleep here, she was going to fall hundreds of feet to the ground below, to almost certain death.

"Great," I muttered to myself. "Life would be so much easier if I were a psychopath."

Even though Bridget had killed two people, I still didn't think she deserved to die, and I didn't want to be the one to kill her. I wanted justice, but that wasn't for me to dole out; it was for the legal system.

"Rhea, goddess mother, attach a cord to this dragon below me."

A rope shot out from my wand and hooked itself around Bridget's paw, above her claws, just as she fell asleep and began plunging toward the ground. As the rope got taught, I suddenly found myself pulled downward as well, the weight of the dragon being far more than what my broom could support.

"Hopefully they put you on a diet in jail," I muttered to Bridget as I struggled to get control of the broom and of the dragon. I pulled upward on the broom as hard as I could, but it was a struggle. We were falling toward the forest below at a much, much faster rate than I was comfortable with, and there was nothing I could do about it.

I could have just let the wand go and let the rope drop Bridget to the ground. But that would have meant certain death for her. This way, there was still a chance for both of us.

"Oh, Rhea," I said as I realized I was going to hit the trees below. "I really don't want to die with my hair looking like this." The rain had not been kind to my appearance. They were going to find my body with hair that looked like long worms.

What? It was *my* deathbed—or more accurately, deathbroom—and I could choose to be vain if I wanted to.

CHAPTER 25

*W*hen I woke up, I groaned.

"Am I dead?" I asked aloud, looking at the sky. It was still raining. That pointed toward my still being among the living. Or did it? I really had no idea.

The pain in my leg definitely gave me a good idea. I paused and looked around. I was lying on the ground in the forest. Crushed twigs were beneath me. My broom lay about ten feet away, cracked in half. I couldn't see my wand, but Bridget lay about thirty feet from me, having taken out a giant fir tree on her way down. Luckily, it had fallen in the opposite direction to me.

I could hear her loud dragon snores from here. She was still alive. We were both alive.

Hobbling to my feet, I was distressed to find myself completely incapable of putting weight on my left foot.

"Shoot," I muttered, looking around for my wand. "Double shoot," I added when I saw it, snapped into three pieces, right where I had been lying a moment earlier. Betrayed by my own butt. How far was I from town?

I pulled out my phone and saw the dreaded words: no service.

On the bright side, because Bridget's nap was magically induced, there was absolutely zero chance she would wake up unexpectedly. She was going to enjoy her rest until someone cast a spell reversing it.

I briefly considered leaving a note just in case someone scampering along the mountainside happened to come across the sleeping dragon and decide to wake her up. But then, I didn't have anything to write "Murderer—probably best to leave her asleep" on, so I figured I was going to have to take my chances.

Finding a piece of wood to lean on, I started limping back toward town. At least, I hoped I was heading toward town. I was halfway up the mountain, so I just started heading downhill. I had no other options, really.

After I made it around fifty feet, I realized it was hopeless. I had one leg, I had no magic, and I was goodness knows how far from town. I ended up making my way back to where I had started and sat back down where I'd fallen.

It probably would have been easier if I'd just died straight away. Now I was wet, I was cold, I had no way

202 | SAMANTHA SILVER

to get home, and I was basically just going to sit here until I eventually succumbed to starvation or something.

"Well, this sucks," I said aloud to the skies. Giant raindrops fell on my face, and I closed my eyes, thinking that maybe if I wished to be back in town, it would happen.

"I can think of better places to have a nap," a familiar voice suddenly said from above me. My eyes sprung open to see Grandma Rosie's face staring down at me.

"I'm injured," I called out. "Get help."

"I am the help," Grandma Rosie said, weaving down toward the ground. She narrowly missed a tree on the way, and I winced, hoping the two of us weren't going to end up injured.

"Didn't the Healers tell you to stop riding a broom, like, ten years ago?" I asked.

"What do those idiots know? Besides, if it weren't for me, you'd still be out here by yourself looking like a drowned rat."

She had a point there.

"How did you find me? How did you even know I was here?"

"I was looking out the window and saw a witch being chased by a dragon. I didn't know who it was but naturally, I wanted to investigate. What if it was linked to the murder investigation? Of course, you mother thought I was making things up, so she wouldn't come have a look."

"So you saw a dragon shooting fire at a witch and figured you'd investigate."

"Your tone implies you're not grateful."

"It's more incredulity. Of everyone in town who might have seen the fight go down, you're the only one who actually came out to have a look. Thanks, Grandma."

"Well, before I help you, you have to tell me why you were fighting the dragon. Is that spell magic?"

I nodded. "Yeah. Please don't try to reverse it. My wand is broken, and she tried to kill me."

"Who is it?"

"I'm absolutely not telling you that."

"I'm not taking you back to town, then."

I strongly considered letting Grandma Rosie go and letting the secret die with me. I was just that spiteful. But then, the odds were Blaze and Anne's killer would go unpunished. And as much as I didn't want to tell Grandma Rosie what I knew, I wanted Bridget to pay for what she'd done. It wouldn't be fair to let her go free.

"It's Bridget."

"Blaze's sister?"

"That's right. She tried to kill me, and I eventually managed to put her to sleep."

Grandma Rosie cackled. "What kind of crazy dragon thinks going up against a *witch* is a good idea?"

"That one, obviously. Now, can we get out of here?"

"Climb on," Grandma Rosie said, motioning to the broom behind her, and I eyed her dubiously.

"Why don't I take the front seat?" I suggested. "You can ride in the back."

"Oh, please. You think I can't fly a broom anymore. Well, I can always leave you here."

"Alright, alright. But I don't have my wand, so please try not to do anything ridiculous."

"Does that sound like the sort of thing I'd do?"

Despite having had a dragon try to kill me, I was fairly certain getting on the broom with Grandma Rosie was actually the most dangerous thing I was going to do today. I hobbled toward her.

"Wow, you look worse than I did before I got that hip replacement," Grandma Rosie said, and I glared at her in reply, managing to swing my bad leg over the broom handle without too much pain and wrapping my arms around Grandma Rosie.

"Hold on!" she said, and I squeezed my eyes shut, determined not to look if I was risking death for a second time in just a few hours.

A few minutes later, I dared to open my eyes and have a peek to see the lights of Mt. Rheanier coming toward me. I almost cried, I was so happy. The adrenaline was wearing off, and I was soaked, terrified freezing, and feeling a whole host of other emotions I couldn't quite identify.

Grandma Rosie, to my surprise and delight

managed to land more or less flawlessly in front of the hospital. She might have nicked one of the trees on the way in, but given how low my standards were, I was considering it a perfect landing.

I hobbled inside, where an assistant Healer immediately spotted me and rushed over with a wheelchair, which I sat in gratefully.

"You look like you've had quite the adventure," she said as she wheeled me down the hall.

"You have absolutely no idea," I replied.

CHAPTER 26

The next few hours flew by in a blur of people and conversations that I barely remembered afterward.

Grandma Rosie must have called Chief Enforcer Loeb, because she arrived right as the assistant Healer brought me a warming potion. As I drank it, warmth spread through every inch of my body, like a warm soup on steroids.

"I'm surprised my grandmother called you," I admitted when I saw the Chief Enforcer.

"Oh?" she said, her eyebrows rising.

"I thought she would have gone to you herself. After all, I know my grandmother is after the reward money."

"Does that mean you know who killed Blaze?"

I nodded and recounted the entire tale, telling Chief Enforcer Loeb that my grandmother could tell her exactly where she could find the sleeping dragon and bring her to justice.

Chief Enforcer Loeb gave me a hard look. "This is why I didn't want the family to put up a reward. I was worried it would lead to a situation just like this one, in which it's a miracle you weren't killed. Even though you didn't know Bridget was the killer when you went to see her, she was the killer, and she went after you."

"Well, all's well that ends well," I replied glibly.

"This time," Chief Enforcer Loeb said, eyeing me seriously with her black eyes. "I'm glad you're safe."

"Not as glad as I am. But thank you."

Just as Chief Enforcer Loeb left the room, her head held high and walking with an elegance I knew I'd never have even with a lifetime of practice, my mother came scurrying past her and into the room.

"Althea! Oh, Althea. My dear daughter, are you alright?"

"I'm fine, Mom, don't worry," I said. "It's just a broken leg. They're making a potion to help repair it faster right now."

"Nonsense. I can't believe you were almost killed. I'm going to go make sure they're making that potion right."

"No, you're not, Mom," I said firmly. I had to admit, I was touched. My mom could be harsh about my life decisions—which, admittedly, could be better a lot of the time—but when it really mattered, she cared more deeply about me than anyone. "The

Healers know what they're doing. It's going to be fine."

"Is Willow here? Willow should be working here. I trust her to make a good potion."

"I don't think so. It's late, and she came over and had an early dinner with me a few hours ago. She's probably at home sleeping."

"Well, they need to call her back in here so she can work on you."

"Mom, no! It's fine. How did you know I was here, anyway?"

"Your grandmother called to gloat. Can you believe that? She wanted to *gloat* that she was right and I was wrong when I said not to go out tonight."

I laughed. That sounded exactly like Grandma Rosie.

"Of course you'd take her side."

"Well, I'm not going to lie, I'm kind of glad she decided to go out," I admitted. "I wasn't looking forward to my impending death by exposure, or worse, starvation."

My mom didn't have an answer to that, but I could see her mouthing a prayer to Rhea.

"Well, I'm glad you're alright. Do you need anything? I can stop by home and get you whatever you need."

I shook my head. "Honestly, I'm exhausted. I think I'm just going to get some sleep."

Mom nodded. "Alright. I'll be here when you wake up."

Mom took my hand as I leaned back and closed my eyes. I found myself sound asleep within seconds.

Who knew near-death experiences were a great sleep aid?

Sure enough, when I woke up the next morning, mom was still there. "They tried to give you the salve last night, but you were sleeping, so I made them wait," she told me. "I'll go let the Healers know you're ready now."

Mom left the room, and a minute later the curtain was pulled back, with Leda and Willow entering the room. Willow had a large cauldron in her hand. I smiled at them both, a weary, grateful smile.

"I'm glad you're not dead," Willow said. "Though from what I hear, it was touch and go for a bit, there."

"Certainly closer than I was comfortable with," I admitted as Leda came over and gave me a big hug.

"I'm so glad you're ok, Ali. Mom only called me this morning to let me know what had happened; she didn't want to wake me up."

"That's fine," I said with a smile. "I mostly just slept last night, anyway. I was pretty sleepy."

Willow began carefully applying paste on my exposed leg, and warmth immediately passed through it.

"This will speed up the healing process, but it still won't be instant. You'll need a cast for about a week.

And we need to catch up. You need to tell me the whole story."

"I will," I promised.

"She needs to rest some more first," Leda said. "Look at her. She's exhausted."

"Right," Willow agreed. "You're staying here for at least another twenty-four hours. Get some rest."

I nodded as the two of them left, Willow promising to bring me by some food that was far more palatable than what the hospital served for lunch.

I drifted in and out of sleep for a while, completely losing track of time. Eventually, however, I woke up and found two dragon shifters standing in front of me. I recognized them; they were Blaze's parents.

"I'm so sorry for your loss," I said. "And I'm sorry for…" I drifted off. How did you apologize for proving their daughter killed their son and was now going to spend the rest of her life in prison?

"Thank you, dear," Blaze's mother said, her eyes watering immediately. She swallowed hard and continued. "Chief Enforcer Loeb came to see us today. As difficult as the news was to hear, we believe it. Bridget was always so concerned with the family, and our reputation, but I never thought she would go to these lengths. Goodness, I can't believe it. That poor witch And, of course, my baby boy."

"Did you have a problem with their relationship?" asked, and Blaze's father grimaced.

"I think we would have come to terms with it even

tually, had we known. We did raise the children to believe that they had to be in a relationship with other dragons only, so I can't help but believe this is partially our fault. I didn't realize we had inadvertently raised Bridget to be so passionate about it."

Blaze's mother began to sob then, and his father took her in his arms. It was a sad sight; I couldn't begin to imagine how they felt. After a moment, Blaze's mother composed herself and pulled a piece of paper out from her purse.

"This is the reward money. We wanted to give it to you. We wanted to thank you for finding our son's killer. It was the worst possible outcome for us, to lose both our children, but for the safety of everyone in town, it is best if Bridget is prevented from ever doing this to anyone again."

I nodded. "Thank you. Blaze was a good dragon. He will be missed."

"Yes, he will," his mother replied in a quiet voice. "I'm glad his killer was found. I'd rather it had been anyone else, but at least now we have some closure."

The two of them left soon afterward, and I opened the paper to find it was, in fact, a check to the tune of half a million abras, made out to me.

The sight of it literally took my breath away. I had never seen that much money in my life.

I shoved it under the pillow and fell back asleep.

When I woke up again, Jack was standing over me, smiling.

"Ugh. Can you take me back out to the forest and leave me to die?" I asked, closing my eyes. Jack just laughed.

"Still mad at me, huh?"

"Take a wild stab in the dark."

"I just wanted to check on you and make sure you're ok. Honestly, I'd have been more worried if you were suddenly nice to me. This all seems par for the course, so I think you're fine."

I threw my pillow across the room at him, then groaned when he easily caught it and refused to give it back. I guess I'd earned that.

"Why didn't you tell me about Andy, anyway?" I shot back. "I thought you and him were together. As in, lovers together."

Jack grinned. "I know. I saw you jump to conclusions faster than LeBron James the instant you saw us."

"Why didn't you say something?"

"I figured it would be more entertaining if you figured it out yourself."

"Yeah, well, joke's on you. You weren't there when I did figure it out and make an idiot of myself," I retorted.

Jack laughed heartily. "Well, at least it happened Anyway, I know you don't want to see me, so now that I know you're fine, I'll leave you alone. Rest up, and let me know if I can do anything for you."

"I won't," I muttered at his back, irrationally annoyed that he wouldn't just hate me back. It wa easier to be mad at someone when they weren't still perfectly nice to you.

*was released a day later, feeling a little bit more rejuvenated, with strict orders from the Healers to rest up and let the leg heal. I figured my brain needed to do a bit of healing, too.

Bridget admitted to everything, I found out, and was going to spend the rest of her life in prison.

Willow popped by every day to bring me food, which I was eternally grateful for, as it was harder than I thought it would be to move from my main living quarters of the couch over to the kitchen. And trying to handle a knife without chopping off a finger while standing on one leg was also more challenging than I had expected. My phalanges were especially grateful for Willow's visits.

"What are you going to do with the money?" Willow asked, and I shrugged.

"So far, I've deposited the check and I've been happily looking at the balance every day," I said with a grin. "But I'm not sure. I want to be able to keep at least half of it so I can buy my mom the kind of house she deserves. You're not allowed to tell her that, though. It's a secret."

Willow motioned a zipper across her lips.

"I think I'm just going to try and keep living frugally

off the rest of it while I try and find another job. Though I am looking forward to my next stab at the magical fixer training role in six months."

Willow smiled. "I think that's a good plan. Take a bit of time to find yourself. And maybe try not to solve any more crimes."

I laughed. "Don't worry. One experience was enough. My crime-solving days are behind me."

Little did I know just how wrong I was.

*B*ook 2: **Get with the Potion:** Ali finally feels like she's got a bit of breathing room in her life. She's got a bit of cash to get by and is just waiting to take the test and embark on her new career. Plus, it helps that she's in everyone's good graces after solving a murder a few weeks earlier.

But when a witch Ali had a run-in with the previous day is found dead, everything changes. Ali finds herself going from local hero to pariah overnight, with the whole town believing her to be the killer. Never one to sit around and wait for things to happen, Ali decides the best way to take charge in this situation is by finding the killer herself, and clearing her own name.

Of course, the list of people who think this is a good idea has exactly one name on it: Ali's. Willow and Leda are sure Ali is going to end up getting arrested - or worse - in the course of this investigation, and Ali keeps on running into that hot new enforcer for some reason, even though she's doing her best to avoid him.

But as Ali digs deeper into the case, with the help of some new friends from Pacific Cove, she realizes not everything is exactly as it seems. Will she be able to get to the bottom of things and solve the case before the killer gets to her first?

Click or tap here to preorder Get with the Potion now – release date November 2nd, 2019

First of all, I wanted to thank you for reading this book. I well and truly hope you enjoyed reading this book as much as I loved writing it.

To be the first to find out about new releases, please feel free to sign up to my newsletter to receive an email every time I release a new book. To sign up for my newsletter, click here now.

If you enjoyed Going Through the Potions I'd really appreciate it if you could take a moment and leave a review for the book on Amazon, to help other readers find the book as well.

Want to read more of Ali's adventures? The second book in the Pacific North Witches Mystery series, Get with the Potion, is now available for preorder on Amazon, set for release on November 2nd, 2019. Click here to preorder it now.

Other Pacific North Witches Mysteries

Get with the Potion (Pacific North Witches #2)

Other books by Samantha Silver

Western Woods Mysteries

Back to Spell One (Western Woods Mystery #1)

Two Peas in a Potion (Western Woods Mystery #2)

Three's a Coven (Western Woods Mystery #3)

Four Leaf Clovers (Western Woods Mystery #4)

Five Charm Fire (Western Woods Mystery #5)

Seven Year Witch (Western Woods Mystery #7)

Behind the Eight Spell (Western Woods Mystery #8)

Magical Bookshop Mysteries

Alice in Murderland (Magical Bookshop Mystery #1)

Murder on the Oregon Express (Magical Bookshop Mystery #2)

The Very Killer Caterpillar (Magical Bookshop Mystery #3)

Death Quixote (Magical Bookshop Mystery #4)

Pride and Premeditation (Magical Bookshop Mystery #5)

Wuthering Homicides (Magical Bookshop Mystery #6)

Willow Bay Witches Mysteries

The Purr-fect Crime (Willow Bay Witches #1)

Barking up the Wrong Tree (Willow Bay Witches #2)

Just Horsing Around (Willow Bay Witches #3)

Lipstick on a Pig (Willow Bay Witches #4)

A Grizzly Discovery (Willow Bay Witches #5)

Sleeping with the Fishes (Willow Bay Witches #6)

Get your Ducks in a Row (Willow Bay Witches #7)

Busy as a Beaver (Willow Bay Witches #8)

Pacific Cove Mysteries

Dark Chocolate and Death (Pacific Cove Witches #1)

White Chocolate and Wands (Pacific Cove Witches #2)

Chocolate Truffles and Trouble (Pacific Cove Witches #3)

Cassie Coburn Mysteries

Poison in Paddington (Cassie Coburn Mystery #1)

Bombing in Belgravia (Cassie Coburn Mystery #2)

Whacked in Whitechapel (Cassie Coburn Mystery #3)

Strangled in Soho (Cassie Coburn Mystery #4)

Stabbed in Shoreditch (Cassie Coburn Mystery #5)

Killed in King's Cross (Cassie Coburn Mystery #6)

Ruby Bay Mysteries

Death Down Under (Ruby Bay Mystery #1)

Arson in Australia (Ruby Bay Mystery #2)

The Killer Kangaroo (Ruby Bay Mystery #3)

Moonlight Cove Mysteries

Witching Aint's Easy (Moonlight Cove Mystery #1)

Witching for the Best (Moonlight Cove Mystery #2)

Thank your Lucky Spells (Moonlight Cove Mystery #3)

A Perfect Spell (Moonlight Cove Mystery #4)

Beat Around the Broom (Moonlight Cove Mystery #5)

California Witching Mysteries

Witches and Wine (California Witching Mystery #1)

Poison and Pinot (California Witching Mystery #2)

Merlot and Murder (California Witching Mystery #3)

ABOUT THE AUTHOR

Samantha Silver lives in British Columbia, Canada, along with her husband and a little old doggie named Terra. She loves animals, skiing and of course, writing cozy mysteries.

You can connect with Samantha online here:
Facebook
Email
Join Samantha Silver's Fantastic Fans reader group on Facebook as well for sneak previews, cover reveals and more!

Made in the USA
Columbia, SC
04 October 2020